I0620272

AA

Aux Arc Novel

(Ozark Novel)

Also by Robert Dean Anderson
LIMB OF THE JUDAS TREE
ASHES-THE YEAR THEY BURNED OLD LINN CREEK
THE BOTTOM OF THE LAKE
THOSE FAREWELL BLUES
THE BANK ROBBER AND THE TEXAS RANGER
GONE-THE TRUE STORY OF THE STEALING OF JESSE PEASTER
DAM OVER TROUBLED WATERS
THE LEFT-HANDED SHORTSTOP
NO WAY TO DIE
THE BOOK OF JOHN

E-BOOKS
LOOKING FOR EL GATO
LIVING AND DYING IN DIXIE
THE WRITER WHO HAS A NOVEL EXPERIENCE
SIDE EFFECTS

THE
SPECIAL
EDITION

Robert Dean Anderson

Copyright © 2014 by Robert Dean Anderson. All rights reserved including the right of reproduction in whole or in part in any form. Published in the United States of America.

First Edition
ISBN 978-0-9720680-5-5

AUTHOR'S NOTE
The individual characters, organizations, corporations and agencies that appear in this book are wholly fictional. None bear any resemblance to any person alive or dead whom I have ever known or encountered. Any apparent resemblance of a character to any person alive or dead, or to any organization, corporation or agency that exists is entirely coincidental.

6

An Aux Arc Novel (Ozark Novel) Published in the United States

For lovable and vastly talented Gwen, who began her newspaper career enthusiastically at the age of eleven and wisely ended it at twenty-one.

Prologue

On a rather typical autumn day that would become like no other, an Arrowhead Truckliner with a thirty foot trailer illegally in tow, crossed the median of State highway 4 and demolished an on-coming van carrying a family of six and overturned onto its side. All six of the van occupants were dead when they reached the hospital in nearby Cluster. The driver of the truck was treated in the hospital for multiple contusions and abrasions. The Highway Patrol called for a wrecker service to remove the truck from the highway shoulder and dispatched a trooper to the hospital to question Gilbert Ramirez, the driver of the truck. The trooper found that Rameriz had been discharged. The hospital had been unable to obtain any pertinent information about the driver whose name had been posted in the truck.

The trooper stationed by the truck to keep traffic moving, stated to his superiors that he had detected a strong odor near the truck and upon looking inside through one of the rear doors that sprung apart, he noted that the truck was stacked to the top with cardboard containers about three foot square and five feet high. He called for an investigator to check the truck's contents, but he was unable to wait for the investigator's arrival after being called to another serious accident five miles away.

When the wrecker that had been called by the first patrolman on the scene arrived they found another service had already set the truck and its trailer upright and the truck was running and preparing to leave the scene. When the investigator who had been summoned to the accident arrived, the late responding wrecker service stated they knew nothing about the service that had dispatched the truck on its way. Nor could they say where the truck or the wrecker service went.

The Patrol traced the truck driver, Gilbert Ramirez, to the town of New Port, twenty miles away in the same county. New Port was also the headquarters terminal for Arrowhead Trucking. When the Patrol sergeant took a request for an arrest warrant to Edward Dunn, the prosecuting attorney for Custer County, it was denied. Three months later when the brother of the father killed with his family in the van filed a civil suit in Custer County against Gilbert Ramirez and Arrowhead Trucking, Judge Harold Turner rejected the suit as lacking in evidence that indicated responsibility for the accident.

Two weeks later, Gilbert Ramirez was transferred to Colorado.

The Cluster County Carrier had one paragraph about the accident, but the New Port newspaper, *The Special Edition*, never carried a story about the accident. Not until sometime after Cooper Rease left prison and became editor.

FREEDOM
OF THE PRESS

"Let the people know the facts, and the country will be safe." Abraham Lincoln

"I get up in the morning and I ask the question: 'What are the bastards hiding?'" Bob Woodward

When he came to the building he immediately thought, "Run-down." The gas pumps that stood in front and had once drew the customers—the only excuse for anyone to stop there—had long since deteriorated. But Cooper Rease could smell them, could smell the petroleum fumes emanating from the soil. He parked his ten-year old Toyota under the portico and sat for a moment, letting the engine idle. The front door, all glass, bore a taped on, hand lettered sign informing him that the business was closed. A smaller sign on the door near the top of the glass was actually the torn-off masthead of the newspaper, *The Special Edition*. So it was true, that was the actual name of the publication. Cooper had doubted or thought he had heard the man incorrectly when he had called about the job.

The door opened and a man of sixties with longish white hair and an immaculately trimmed goatee and mustache stood there. He motioned with a hand, a gesture Cooper interpreted as an invitation to come inside. He shut off the Toyota, got out and approached the man saying, "Mister Graham?"

The man stuck out his hand, shook Cooper's hand and waved him inside.

"Reese?" the man asked. "Like the peanut butter candy bar?"

"With nuts," Cooper said, thinking are we going to start this transaction on a joke?

Graham wasn't laughing. "I did some checking. You just got out of prison."

So that was out of the way. "I did some stupid things," Cooper said. "While you were doing the checking I hope you checked with the *Kansas City Star* about my work before my trouble."

"I did," Graham said. He had Cooper caught in his stare. "That's why you're here."

Cooper waited, then said, "I did some checking, too. You've been trying to sell this paper for three years. It's a dead newspaper in a dying town. You own the paper twenty miles up the road in Cluster and you've been trying to sell it. You haven't had an editor here for a year. They tell me at the Press Association you've been using filler and ads that nobody pays for just so you don't lose your second class mailing permit."

Graham, still with the stare, said, "All true. You think that about the paper, why'd you come?"

"I've got ties here."

Graham broke the stare, waved his hand in the air and said, "Well, what the hell. The damn paper can't go much lower than it is now. People think about an ex-con as editor and they get a laugh out of it. It's pretty much a joke around the county anyway. I'll give you two thousand a month salary and I own a mobile home down the street you can have rent free."

"I want an option to buy," Cooper said.

"You have any money?"

"I'll have a couple thousand in a few months. I hear you own the restaurant at the truck stop. I'll take my meals there. Part of the deal."

14

The Special Edition

Graham broke into a slight grin. "I can arrange that. Drinks don't go with it. I heard you had a drinking problem."

"Operative word is *had*."

"I'll draw up the papers," Graham's hand came out of his pocket with a ring of keys. "Here's the key to the mobile home and to the door here. You got a desk in here and three computers, a couple of printers and a scanner. Telephone. All you'll need. We've been printing the paper at Cluster. You can e-mail the paper to us on Tuesday. We'll deliver four hundred copies to you here Wednesday morning. You've got a labeler there. Shouldn't be any problem. You miss getting a paper in the mail and you're gone. We can only miss twice a year or we lose the permit."

"What about help?" Cooper asked.

"Help? With an eight page tabloid you need help?"

"I'm assuming you want to improve and expand the paper so it will be worth more. Isn't that's why you wanted an editor?"

"All right, I'll make it twenty-five hundred a month. You want any help, take it out of that."

"Make it three thousand," Cooper said.

The stare was back. Finally, "All right then. Tomorrow's Wednesday. You'll get four hundred papers before noon and a copy of the contract. Sign it and give it back to the woman who delivers the papers."

Cooper stuck out his hand and Graham took it. He said, "You stay sober and work out I'll put your name in the paper as editor next month."

2

He saw her ride up on an old kick-start, silver tanked, British made Triumph motorcycle, and watched her climb off. She was less than five feet off the ground and weighed in at two digits. Her hair was midnight hued and her eyes nearly as dark. She came through the door of the nineteen-thirtyish gas station building holding a copy of the latest issue of the *Special Edition.* When Cooper looked up she said, "You the man to see about this sticker ad on the paper?"

Cooper recognized the ad on the paper she held as the one he'd printed on label stickers and put on the papers the woman had delivered the day before. The ad read, PART TIME POSI-TION FOR PROLIFIC COMPUTER EXPERT AND AD SALES PERSON. He nodded at the young woman, trying to figure her age. Somewhere around twenty, he guessed.

"How much does it pay?"

"Ten dollars an hour for the work here in the office. Half of all the ad sales you get at four dollars a column inch."

She was quick to compute that and said, "That's pretty good pay. How many hours?"

"No more than twenty, probably. If you sell a lot of ads, you'll get more hours laying them out."

She nodded her head. "I'm Serena Gonzalez. I'd like to apply for the job."

The Special Edition

"Are you legal, Serena?"

"This doesn't have anything to do with sex, does it?"

He tried to figure out what she was getting at.

"Look," he said, "all I want is someone to help put the newspaper out."

"Okay," she said, nodding her head again. "Just checking."

"You're Latino. I'm not supposed to be hiring anyone who doesn't have the right papers."

"My parents brought me here when I was six. They run the nursery and fruit and vegetable store at the edge of town."

He thought about it, then stood up from the chair he'd had to reinforce with two sawed-off two by fours. He waved a hand at the chair and said, "Sit there and let's see how long it takes you to find out everything you can about Cecilia Roth, born December 2, 1967 in Kansas City, Missouri."

She gave him a look, then came around the table which was really an interior house door propped on two saw horses. She sat in the chair looking almost childlike because of her lack of size. She ran the cursor across the tool bar on the desktop, went through a number of rapid keystrokes, clicked through four websites on Google, on through five or six links—doing it so quickly Cooper lost count. She copied lines he didn't have time to read, looking over her shoulder. In what Cooper figured was no more than two minutes, she had several pages—three at least—of a Word document on Cecilia Roth. Cooper reached over her hands and scrolled down the pages reading rapidly.

"Pretty good," he said. "Damn good."

"I go to college Monday, Wednesday and Friday from six to nine in the evening. I won't be able to work those days after five."

"Hmm. Should be okay. Now, make up an ad for the

17

Farmer's Seed store on the edge of town."

"I know the place," she said. She thought for a moment, then scrolled through the applications on the computer, picked one, opened it and asked, "What size?"

"Make it a five inch by eight inch.That's a two column by eight inch ad, 16 column inches, sixty four dollars."

She drew in a border, searched for clip art, copied a cartoon figure smiling and holding a handful of carrots and wrote in the caption, "YOU HAVE TO PLANT THEM TO HARVEST THEM. GET YOUR SEEDS AND FERTILIZER AT FARM-ERS SEED STORE. HALF PRICE THIS SATURDAY ONLY." She clicked on PRINT and out came two copies of the ad."

"Pretty good," Cooper said, holding one in his hand. "We should have a logo for them, but I couldn't find any on file . . ."

Before he finished talking she had clicked enough keys to bring up a logo for the store. She copied it, placed it on the ad and ran off two more copies.

"Pretty good," he said again. "If you can go out and sell it to them, you've got the job."

"I don't make the coffee," she said.

"I'll teach you."

She did a thing with her mouth indicating contemplation, which morphed into a slight grin.

"I get mileage?"

He looked through the grease and dust smeared window at the old Triumph motorcycle she had ridden there.

"Five cents a mile," he said.

"IRS gives more than forty."

"I'm not IRS."

She folded the ad sheets and slipped them in the hip pocket

of her skin tight jeans which Cooper thought must be about a size two, and left out the door. He watched her straddle the Triumph, jump on the starter, twist the engine into a roar, kick up the stand with feet clad in long, leather boots and roar away, all in a singular motion. Cooper was impressed.

She was back in fifteen minutes. She unfolded the ad sheet and handed it to him. Written on the bottom was an agreement to place the ad in the next eight issues at sixty-four dollars each and one in the ninth issue free of charge. A signature at the bottom of the agreement Cooper assumed to be the owner of the Farmers Seed Store.

"This free ad," Cooper said, "that was his idea?"

"Mine," she said.

He pursed his lips and nodded. He looked at the ad again, at the first sold ad in the paper he was the editor of. "When can you start?"

"I figure I started an hour ago," she said, grinning slightly.

"So you did."

"One question," she said. He waited. "Why Cecilia Roth?"

"My mother," he told her.

"Says she was murdered. Right here in New Port, three years ago."

"That's right."

"Your name was in the ad you stuck on the front of the paper. Wasn't in the list of survivors."

"My brother wrote the obituary. We aren't that close." He paused while she thought about that. "And I was in prison."

"What did you do?"

"Assault. I hit the prosecutor in court."

"Why?"

"I refused to reveal a source on an article I wrote for the *Kansas City Star*. He lied about me in court and called me a hack."

She looked around. "Where's my desk?"

"I'll have to put one together for you."

She walked around his make-shift table and sat in his reinforced chair again. "I'll sit here until you get it ready," she said and had her hands on the keyboard clicking on files again.

Cooper wondered who was now in charge.

3

Cooper's first issue of the *Special Edition* contained fourteen ads that were actually paid for. Serena put in thirty hours that week—wiping out all the income off the ads she sold—but she had ended up writing more column inches of news than he had. She knew everyone in and around New Port and she gathered the local news like a vacuum. Cooper, on the other hand, hit a lot of stone walls when he when he went through the city offices and the county offices trying to pry out information.

Graham called to tell him that the issue had lost eight hundred dollars.

"Maybe more," Cooper said. "I sold the ads for two dollars an inch."

"That makes it about a thousand dollars I lost," Graham said. "I should have put you on a commission. Hell, if I'd wanted to give the damn ads away why would I be paying you?"

"How many ads did you actually sell in the last issue before I started?" Cooper asked.

"Yeah, I know. I'll probably never collect off them. How you going to collect off the ones you sold?"

"I hired an ad sales person. She'll collect."

"Aw," Graham said, "now I get it. You hired that fruit picker's kid, that Mexican girl, didn't you? That's why people been calling me asking about her. I wondered. Seems she kinda rubs people raw sometimes in case you hadn't found that out yet."

"This paper did better than the one before it," Cooper told him. "That's what you hired me for, wasn't it?"

"Okay," Graham said. "It's better, but I'm still losing money on it. I'm going to have to modify our agreement slightly. I'll give you six weeks to put the damn thing on a paying basis or I'm killing it."

"You want a better paper or not?"

"What I'm wantin' and what I'm gettin' haven't come together yet."

"Gotta go," Cooper said and hung up the phone.

Serena had come in with a handful of ads and had listened to the end of his conversation with Graham.

"Hate to tell you this," she said, "but Mister Graham can't be trusted."

She came around the All Metal used gray steel desk he had gotten in trade with the used furniture store—a full page ad for the desk and a wobbly steel swivel chair—and sat. "I've got twenty-four ads for next week plus the ones you gave away for the desk and chair and for the coffee pot and refrigerator. I tried the grocery store, but they said they had a deal with you for the week's groceries."

Cooper flipped through the ads she had brought in. He stopped at a half-page ad from the used car dealer on Main Street that people called Bilbo. He looked at her. "Look at the next one," she said. He turned the sheet to see a full page ad from a used car dealer in Cluster.

"Showed it to Bilbo, I bet. Clever," he said. "Graham says he has trouble collecting from advertisers here in New Port. That's going to be part of your job. Collecting on the ads you sell."

She opened the back pack she had laid on the desk and took out a small purse. She dumped the contents of the purse on the desk. All money, various denominations.

"You collected in advance?" he asked.

"Just from the deadbeats."

"How did you know which ones that would be?"

"I asked my parents."

"How much did you make last week?"

Without taking time to think about it she said, "A little over six hundred dollars."

"More than I made," he said.

She said nothing audible, but her face said, "So what?"

She did say, "You working on the murders?"

His eyebrows went up. "The murders?"

"There's been seven of them since Soldano Chemicals and Arrowhead Trucking came to town. No arrests. So far."

"New Port doesn't have a police force, I found out. They pay the county and the sheriff does the enforcement. Sheriff Burnett is in the county seat in Cluster. He's never in when I call on him."

"He's a drunk. Peddles drugs. Stay away from him."

Cooper again was feeling as if he wasn't in charge. "How about putting some information together about all these murders," he said. She pulled open a top drawer in her desk and handed him a sheaf of papers. He thumbed through them, seven sheets. A different murder on each sheet. He glanced at her, expecting a smirk, but she looked steadily at him, no expression on her face.

"I get the feeling I don't know you," he said.

"I've heard that before."

Grant Borden was the first of the seven people murdered in the New Port area in the three-year killing spree. Borden was an eighty-four year old widower who owned the land next to Cooper's mother's ten acre plot. Cecilia Roth was mentioned in the article Serena copied because, according to the *Special Edition*, she had told Sheriff Burnett she heard shots the night Borden died inside his burned house. The coroner found two bullet holes in Borden's skull. His death would have been the first murder in Cluster County in sixty-one years, according to the *Special Edition*, if Prosecutor Edward Dunn hadn't pronounced the cause of death as self-inflicted gun shots.

Lou Magliole, a neighbor on the other side of Cecilia Roth, was found dead by his wife a week later. Magliole was lying on his stomach in a field two hundred yards from his house. A shotgun with one empty shell in the chamber was under his body with the barrel under his chin where the shot had entered his head. His wife said Magliole had never owned a shotgun. The death was listed as an accidental self-inflicted gunshot. Two months before hunting season.

Cecilia Roth. Found by her friend Elsie Loring. Cooper's mother had been sexually violated, beaten and left to suffer and die in her bed with her throat slashed. Elsie Loring apparently told the sheriff she had found words written in Cecilia Roth's blood on the sheets of the death bed according to the *Special Edition* story along with a four sentence obituary. The *Cluster County Carrier* had a three sentence report of the crime Sheriff Burnett had investigated and blamed on a passing vagrant. What Elsie Loring told the sheriff was repeated in the *Jefferson City Tribune* where Cooper had read about his mother's death in prison. A week after Cecilia was brutally murdered in her own home, Elsie Loring was killed on Main Street in New Port by a hit and run driver a witness had said was a dark imported sedan with out-of-state license plates different in color from local plates.

Jose Rodriquez was shot in the head inside his Arrowhead Truck semi in a truck stop just inside the Custer County line. Walter Clipton was the latest reported murder in Custer County. He was employed by the Soldano Industry farm that raised hogs. The Soldano farm was a massive swine feeding operation that occupied 3200 acres in the county including the properties that had belonged to Borden, Magliole and Cecilia Roth. Sheriff Burnett said Clipton was killed by a rampaging boar.

Cooper laid the sheets on his house-door table. Serena was pecking away on her iMac, then, noticing he had stopped reading and was staring at her, she said, "Read them all?"

"Six of them. You said seven."

"Man by the name of Martin Dinsmore. Found dead in his car outside the courthouse in Cluster. Cause of death listed as heart attack by the coroner. High levels of unspecified chemicals in his blood stream. Coroner said it could have come from medication, like Warfarin. Rat poison."

"Never reported in either newspaper."

"Right."

"The state never investigated any of these deaths?"

"Sure. No resolution. Soldano Industries is a big backer of the governor."

"So this paper stopped carrying all the reports of the murders. Why?"

She did a thing with her mouth that indicated he should have figured that out by himself. "Woman named Allen. She was the editor, then she wasn't. Nobody knows where she went."

"Maybe she's number eight."

"Maybe."

"How much of this did you already know and how much did you have to look up?"

"I knew most of it."

"What's with the Soldano Farm?" he asked.

"They came in, bought up a bunch of farms and started a huge hog feeding complex. Stinks out there."

"Soldano Industries? I thought they were a chemical company in St. Louis."

"Yeah. They make the seed corn, soy beans, cotton, what have you. The genetically modified stuff."

"And they're in the hog feeding business?"

"They own Arrowhead Trucking also."

"So you're saying what? They feed the hogs the genetically modified grain, haul the meat out on Arrowhead Trucking? And they murdered my mother and those other people to get their farms? Why would they do that? If they wanted their farms, why not deal with the farmers instead of killing them? If they didn't want to sell their farms why didn't they go somewhere else? Lots of farms for sale."

She shrugged.

"And they bought off the sheriff and the other county officials and the governor so they could kill anyone in their way?"

Another shrug.

"You know what bothers me the most about this?"

She didn't ask, but her eyes did.

"Why the hell didn't the people in this damn county do something about it."

"We were waiting for someone like you," she said.

Sheriff Walker Burnett's appearance was not what Cooper expected. His reputation made him seven feet tall and 300 pounds. In person he was less than six feet and topped out near 160, but wiry. Cooper had supposed him to be not available as he had been the last three times Cooper had stopped by his office in the courthouse in Cluster.

The sheriff looked up from his desk, his face a blank. He waited for Cooper to explain his presence.

"Sheriff Burnett?" Cooper asked. The sheriff continued to stare at him without replying. "I'm Cooper Rease. The *Special Edition* down in New Port."

Continued stare.

"I came by to get the incident reports for the last two weeks for publication," Cooper said. "We'll be publishing them weekly from now on. I or my assistant will be dropping by every Monday to copy them."

"The only reports we have in my office are closed to the public," the sheriff said, his voice not harsh or strident. More like a parent to an inquisitive child.

"You're aware of the state's open meetings and publications law," Cooper said.

"Of course."

"Then you're aware that incident reports of duly elected and appointed law enforcement officials are considered open to the press and as a legal matter of fact, the files are open to the public."

"Not by me."

"Are you going to give me a hard time?" Cooper asked.

"Not if you obey the laws of our state and county," the sheriff's tone still the correcting parent.

"How about if *you* obey the laws?"

"Always do."

Cooper reached inside his jacket and took out a folded sheaf of papers and laid them on the desk in front of the sheriff. He pointed with his finger to a yellow high-lighted sentence on the top sheet. "Right there," he said. "Incident reports are open to the public. Read it."

"I have my own copy," the sheriff said, still calm.

"Apparently your copy has not been ratified by the legislature. All files are open except the ones that are under investigation."

"All my files are under investigation. Now, if you'll excuse me, I have work to do for the county." He picked up some papers from a metal file-basket and proceeded to thumb through them.

Cooper waited, thinking about it then, "Okay, everybody I've talked with says you're a real hard ass. So am I. The next time we talk will be in my office."

He left without the sheriff looking up.

Prosecuting Attorney Edward Dunn, a tall and long-limbed man with a hatchet face was in his receptionist's office when Cooper entered. A woman there looked through several open drawers in a row of triple-drawer metal file cabinets. Dunn leaned against one of the cabinets and looked at Cooper, knowing, of course, who he was.

"Mister Dunn?" Cooper asked and the man nodded his elongated head topped by a small gathering of white hair that pointed in all directions.

Cooper introduced himself, then told Dunn the reason for his visit. "Sheriff Burnett refuses to abide by the requirements of the state's open meeting law. The Sunshine Law. When a public official refuses to comply, the law allows for a penalty. I'm filing a complaint against him."

"I see," Dunn said. "Well, I'm sure if the sheriff doesn't allow his records to be open to the public he has a perfectly legal reason for it."

"Why would you be sure of that?"

"Well," Dunn drew himself up to his full height, six inches over Cooper's head, "I've worked with Sheriff Burnett for eight years. I know him quite well and he's a competent law enforcement officer. You, on the other hand, I've not met before today."

"So you've taken an oath to only enforce the law for people you have known for eight years?"

"I've been elected twice by the people of Cluster County, sir. I guess they trust me and my judgment on matters affecting this county."

Cooper, holding the rolled up sheets containing the Sunshine laws for the state, slapped them lightly against his open palm, then said, "It's worse in this county than I have heard it to be. What it is is a confederacy of dunces."

He walked to the office door, opened it, turned back, said, "That's a book. Read it sometime."

The Special Edition

Graham was on the phone asking why in hell Cooper had all the blank spaces in the paper he had e-mailed to the *Carrier* for printing.

"Notice the headings," Cooper said. "Information from elected county officials Nada. Nothing. So, that's what I'm telling the people of New Port that their servants they're paying to do their job, aren't."

"That's not a good way to start off on a good relationship," Graham said. "I'll go ahead and put some filler in there in place of your white spaces."

"You do and I quit and so does Serena. Did you count the ads she sold this week? Did you notice we had to go to 12 pages?"

Graham was silent for a minute, then, "Look, son, what you're doing is stirring up a hornet's nest when there's no need to. You got some good stuff in here about the church suppers and the track meet at the school. That's what people want to read. Not a bunch of liberal rabble-rousing that accuses people."

Cooper said, "Mister Graham. You call yourself a newsman. When did you lose your way?"

He hung up the phone.

Serena came in on her Triumph, kicked the stand down and crawled off, came inside with a handful of sold ads, and saw Cooper stuffing papers into his briefcase. He looked up, at the question on her face, and said, "I'm pulling out for now. Graham won't print the paper we sent him so I'm going to have to do this another way."

"What other way?" she asked.

"I'm going to have to start my own paper."

"You hiring any help?"

He stopped stuffing the papers in his briefcase and looked

fully at her, at her air of unbelieving. Today she appeared to be more than the teenage wizard he'd hired. She was bigger today, somehow. She was his measure and he was cowered by the sudden change she had sprung on him.

Fumbling through his thoughts, he found what he needed to tell her, what he was obligated to confess: "I did something I had no right to do. I told Graham if he didn't print the paper the way we sent it to him, we were both quitting. I didn't have the right to include you. Call him, he'll keep you on, especially with all the ads you're bringing in."

"Never took you for a quitter."

Through the grimy window he tried to find a solution for the situation. Not his Toyota, not her Triumph. They represented retreat. He expelled a great breath. "Dammit, I need a drink." He looked at her. "How about you?"

"Falling off the wagon?"

"Will you catch me?"

Now she smiled. "You're still the boss."

The Toyota wouldn't start. Dead battery. Serena invited him to sit behind her on the Triumph.

"Shouldn't I be wearing a helmet?" he asked.

"Helmets are for sissies," she told him, buckling on her own helmet as she fired up the cycle and steered them onto the street. Without asking, she knew where his mobile home was. Cooper kind of liked holding onto her slim waist on the way there. He had never seen the need to lock the door so he waved her to go on inside. He had a six pack with one gone in the small refrigerator. He handed her one and she screwed the top off and took a swig.

The Special Edition

He took his and dropped into the worn recliner as she settled on the lumpy sofa.

"Crummy digs, but it's free," he said and took a drink. She sat forward on the very front of the sofa cushion, elbows on her knees, bottle in her left hand. Was she left handed? He hadn't noticed. He pointed to the Budweiser she held. "Never noticed. You left handed?"

She didn't answer the question. "If you buy the paper or if you start one, I don't want the ten dollars an hour until you break even after your take. Half the ads is enough,"

"You're staying with me, then?"

"If I do, I'd like to hear you say you're not giving up until those murders are solved."

"I never give up," he said. He took a drink, then added, "I've been fired a couple of times. I worked for a small daily in Texas. Had a deal where they were clear-cutting timber on public lands. And the public got nothing out of it. Big outfit doing the cutting. Paid off the publisher who killed the story I was working on. I waited until the publisher took off on vacation and left me in charge. I ran the story. Two people in city hall went to jail, the timber cutter got sued for a million and a half and I got fired when the publisher got back from vacation."

She took a drink and he could tell she was no beer drinker.

"I've got a couple of Dr. Peppers in the fridge if you'd rather," he said. She returned his smile.

"Good newspeople are hard drinkers, I've heard someplace," she said, smiling back at him. "Have to get in practice."

"Is that what you want to be, a newsperson?"

"I've got lots of time to decide that," she said.

"You know, I don't even have a personnel file on you. I don't know your full name, your age, I do know your gender. I'm supposed to withhold taxes, social security, all that stuff on you."

"I'll start a file for you tomorrow," she said, took another drink and tried to suppress a grimace. "I'll need to start a file on you, also. You'll have to tell me all that about you."

He hesitated. How much to tell, how much not to tell. What the hell, he decided, tell it all.

"I was born in the East Texas woods twenty-seven years ago. Went to the university in this state, journalism school. Father and mother separated when I was seven. I went to live with my father, my younger brother went with my mother. I didn't see her again until I was twelve. I told her I hated her. Last time I ever cried. She came to my college graduation and kissed my cheek. My father once called her a whore. I don't know if she was one or not. She ended up on this little farm where she was killed. I never knew anymore than that about her."

He realized how he'd been rushing his words with short sentences. He took several deep breaths. "My dad worked for Haliburton's Blackstone in Iraq. He was one of the private service people who killed a group of Iraqis. They needed a goat and he was chosen. He was serving time for that but he's out now. On to some spy mission or something. He's as tough as they come. Once, I thought I was like him, but I'm not. I already told you how I ended up fired by the *Kansas City Star* and went to the slammer for punching the prosecutor in court. That's more than you need to know and more than I've talked since I was nine."

She smiled at that. "I'm nineteen. I love fooling around on the computer. I love mystery novels the old guys wrote, Elmore Leonard, Robert Parker, Richard Stark. I fantasized about solving the murders myself. I almost had sex when I was fifteen with a boy my age, but he got too nervous to do it. You probably didn't want to hear about that, but you told me about yourself and that's something I've never told anyone before."

He laughed, tried to stop, looked up at her to apologize, that he didn't mean anything, but she was laughing with him. The first time he had ever seen her laugh.

She lifted the bottle, looked at it, laughed some more and said, "I feel light headed."

He had another beer and what was left of Serena's while she drank a Dr. Pepper. They shared a bag of chips and some salsa out of his refrigerator and saw the woman drive by the mobile home bringing the copies of the *Special Edition* to the old gas station office. They rode the Triumph back to the office where Cooper said he was going to throw the papers in the dumpster. The paper on top of the first bundle he picked up looked unlike any newspaper he had ever seen. The front was covered with empty column space.

"I'll be damned," he said. "The bastard printed it like I told him to."

The two of them put the labels on and Serena rode him to the old Western Auto store—that wasn't Western Auto any longer, but hadn't taken down the sign—where he got a battery for the Toyota with some of the money Serena had collected for prepaid ads. He loaded the papers in the Toyota to take them to the post office and Serena straddled her Triumph, called to him before he shut the door to the office and asked, "You staying with the *Special Edition*, then?"

"Unless I get fired or unless he doesn't print my copy."

"See you tomorrow, then," she said and kicked the Triumph to life and rode off.

Throughout the next day a total of twenty people came in to subscribe to the *Special Edition*.

The next week in the Cluster County Courthouse for Cooper was much the same as the week before. None of the county officials were available to him. No one knew when they might be available. Entering the courthouse he noticed that someone had posted the front page of the *Special Edition* with the empty columns on a bulletin board inside the front door. When he left the building the paper had been taken down.

New subscriptions came in during the week. Serena had taken over the bookkeeping as well as the Human Resources job without Cooper asking.

"Forty-one new subscriptions," she told him without looking up from her computer when he returned. "You figure on printing empty columns again?"

"Not on the front page. Guy I met on the street told me he was filing suit against the hog farm. Said three other people had filed one before him, but the judge dismissed them. Lack of evidence. So, the guy brought in a specialist in odors. Olfactory investigator he called him. Says it stinks like hog shit all over the county."

"So you're going out to the hog farm to investigate for yourself?"

"Want to come along?"

"No thanks, the smell stays in your nose for days.."

Serena was right about the smell. He knew the general direction for the hog farm and began to pick up the rank odor before he got to the arching brick and iron entrance with the gate across the drive. The arch over the gate contained the words: SOLDANO AGRICULTURAL FARM. A speaker was mounted on the driver's side of the entry. Cooper rolled down his window and pushed the button below the perforated speaker. A voice answered, "Soldano Farm. What can I do for you"

"Cooper Rease of the *Special Edition*," he said, waited a moment and added, "like to do a story on the farm. Take some pictures of the pigs, that sort of thing."

"Who authorized this?" the voice wanted to know.

"No one, yet. Check with the manager. I won't need to take up much of his time."

The voice was silent long enough that Cooper began to think he was being ignored. The gate started slowly sliding open and the voice directed Cooper to proceed up the hill and straight on to barn number two. "Has a number on the front," the voice told him.

Cooper drove through the gate, up the hill and stopped where he had been directed to stop, by barn number two. A string of glistening, high-priced autos were lined up in front, all behind a long, black Hummer limo. Before he closed the door to the Toyota after getting out he counted sixteen barns in a row. The smell of fresh hog manure was oppressive.

A young man with hard-jaws shaded with dense whiskers, closely-shaved, stood at the door, arms folded, looking at Cooper, saying, "Yes?"

"Cooper Rease, *Special Edition*."

The man looked at Cooper's Canon EOS hanging around his

neck. "Wait," the man said and disappeared inside the barn. Cooper waited.

The man reappeared and held the door open waving Cooper inside with one hand. A group of well dressed men and one woman stood in the center aisle inside the barn. A big man wearing a buckskin jacket with fringe down each arm, an expensive white shirt under it and a Texas-style belt buckle, shiny stone in the center, came forward, hand extended.

"Ev Miehle, buddy," in a hearty tone, "always glad to see the press. What paper you with?"

"New Port's *Special Edition*," Cooper said, taking the man's hand and feeling the strength in it.

"Glad you could come out," the man said. "Marla got to you, huh?"

Cooper didn't answer right away, but the woman, fortyish, short, obviously dyed hair swept back, retro-style black-rimmed fiftyish glasses, said to the Ev Miehle, "That wasn't the name I contacted, Ev."

Miehle waved it off. "Doesn't matter." To Cooper, "You're here to do a piece on the operation, right? Pictures, all that?"

"I'd like to talk about it, yes," Cooper said.

Miehle took him by the arm and started directing him down the aisle. The woman and the two other men fell in behind. The men were both dressed in suit and tie and looked a bit out of place in a hog farrowing barn.

"We've got nine thousand pigs in this operation," Miehle said. "Each barn holds fifty sows and maybe half a thousand piglets. If we're lucky. Only got five boars to service the fifty sows." He jabbed Cooper in the ribs with his elbow, looked at him with a big grin "Lucky boars, huh?" Finished with a laugh."We started in three years ago with ten sows. We raise about a quarter of the feed they eat, buy the rest. Good for the farmers in the area. You smell the hog shit, I imagine. Well, we're working on that. The manure is washed out of the barns twice a day. Goes into two large ponds. Water's filtered before it's run off into the river. Water's tested twice a week. Pure as rain water. All kinds of environmental people went over everything. Got a hundred percent approval from them. We sell the hogs to a place in Omaha that butchers them, ships meat all over the world."

"Impressive," Cooper said. "How'd you get into hog farming?"

"Started with Soldano. You've heard of them, I suppose. Developed these seeds that produced plants immune to the herbicides. Tested the hell out of them, had to have something to do with the grain, see if it was safe for humans so we fed it to hogs, tested the meat, turned out okay. We were stuck with the hog farm so I got the idea we'll make some money out of it."

"Why this location?"

Miehle took a quick look at Cooper. "Why? Hell, I don't know. The whole deal was my idea. My brother Ernest is the serious one. We're partners in Soldano, but we compete in everything else. He's into technology, crap like that. Does well, though. Me, I'm into things people have to have to live. People got to have food, water, air and shelter to live. But, you know what, my best investment is in toilet paper. Can you believe it. I beat old Warren Buffett to that. We grew up on a farm in Minnesota wiping our butts on Sears catalogs. No offense, but newspapers didn't make good ass wipe. Damn ink rubbed off to turn your ass black. It was a relief when we graduated to running water, a flush toilet and toilet paper."

He turned to smile hugely at the woman, Marla. "Ain't that right, Marla? Nice soft toilet paper is a necessity nowadays."

"Sure is, Mr. Miehle," Marla said grim faced.

"Here's a sow right here just popped out a litter of eight," Miehle said, walking up to the chainlink fence dividing the small area where a mother pig lay on the straw-layered floor with little pigs sucking nourishment from her. "Make a good picture, you want one," Miehle said, backing up to the enclosure and turning toward Cooper. Cooper aimed his Canon and shot off several shots of the smiling Miehle with the sow and pigs in the background.

"Send me a copy of the paper when you print it," he said. "I'll send it on to Ernest. He's a stuffed shirt. Wouldn't be caught dead inside a hog barn."

Cooper said, "I understand the Miehle brothers are big political contributors."

"We're big contributors to every damn thing, Everybody's got their hand out. Damn politicians line up before election. We give to both sides, more to the ones that don't want to tax us to death. But, hell, old Warren's right about taxes. We ought to be paying more than guys like you. Old Ernest, he don't give a dime to the liberals. He as hard ass as you can get when it comes to politics. Me, I'd rather be out here on the hog farm than in some damn political gabfest."

"I hear you've been sued several times over the smell coming from the hogs," Cooper said, marveling at how forward the man was.

"Yeah, can't say I blame them. I just go ahead and buy them out. Cheaper than going through court." He turned to one of the men behind him in a suit, a blond, stern faced young man of thirty or less. "Ain't that right, Carson?" He turned back to Cooper. "Carson's my lawyer for today. Watch him, he'll sue your ass off if he don't like the story you print." Miehle laughed heartily and slapped Cooper on the back. "I guess I'm like the old Texas rancher they talk about. Said he didn't want all the land in Texas, just that part next to his."

"Is that how you got the land for the hog farm?"

"Damned if I know. I think we bought it through the bank." He turned to the other man in a suit standing beside Carson and carrying a briefcase. "Miller, who'd we buy the farm here from?"

Miller said, "State Bank in Kansas City."

"Yeah?" Miehle said, "Did we get a good deal?"

"A little over average farm acreage," Miller said.

"Yeah? You overpaid? Maybe I ought to fire you," Miehle laughed again. "Listen, Cooper was it? I've got to leave. Look over some timber in the south part of the state. That's what we make the toilet paper from, you know. I'll turn you over to Carson. He can fill you in on the rest of your questions and interview. I don't need him anymore, anyway. I understand he's got another lawsuit been filed against us. Right Carson? Take care of it."

Miehle was moving away when he put his hand out for a quick shake of Cooper's hand. He walked rapidly toward the front of the barn, turned back, still on the move, and said, "Don't forget to send me a copy. Carson will give you the address."

The woman Marla and the man Miller followed Miehle out the door.

Cooper and Carson stood watching them leave. Carson, smiling, looked at Cooper. "What else would you like to know?"

"Who killed the three people who used to own this farm?"

Carson was having trouble with Cooper's question. "What people? What do you mean, killed?"

"Grant Borden, Leo Magliole and Cecilia Roth. Their three farms became part of this farm after they were killed. No one has been arrested for their murders." Cooper had stopped just inside the barn door to face Carson who stood with one hand on the door, half turned toward Cooper.

"What are you saying? Is there an accusation in that question?"

"Just a question," Cooper said. "The record is pretty clear. Look it up. Borden burned up in his house fire with two bullet holes in his head. Magliole shot with a shotgun he didn't own. Cecilia killed by an intruder. Maybe. Maybe not."

"Who says they were murdered?" Carson getting testy.

"I do. I read the news articles on them."

"The property, as I understand it, was purchased through a bank in Kansas City, They would be the ones to answer your question."

"Okay," Cooper nodded and walked past Carson through the door to the outside. "I have a few more questions and that will wrap it up."

"As long as they're not accusations," Carson said.

Cooper went to work on his article after downloading the photos he had taken at the hog farm. He liked the one where Ev Miehle posed in front of the sow and pigs and made that his front page shot, three columns wide. He was nearly through his story when Serena returned, hands full of ads.

"Phew," she said. "You've been to the hog farm."

"Got a hot story," Cooper said, not looking up from his computer. "Shower later."

Serena went to her All-Metal desk, hit some keys on the keyboard that started the printer humming. She pulled the sheets and laid them on Cooper's house-door table. "Read that," she said.

He glanced at the papers, looked at her, said, "Where did you get this?"

"Someone dropped it in our mailbox out front."

"You mean . . .?"

"Anonymous. We have a friend in the courthouse."

Cooper picked it up and read the heading: "Incident Report, Sheriff's office. Last week."

"Empty columns minus one," Serena said. "There's some dandies in there."

Cooper started reading, started smiling, looked up, "These are priceless. In the words of the investigating officers. I couldn't make this stuff up. Listen to this one, the woman came across the street and bit the head off the neighbor kid's pet frog."

"It's good," Serena agreed. "Are you going to run this next week?"

"How do we know this is authentic?"

"I checked on a couple of them. Names and addresses were included so I called the people or called their neighbors. The four I checked on were correct."

Cooper nodded. "Good job, Serena." He continued to look at her. "You're amazing, you know it?"

Serena looked down, embarrassed. "My dog loves me," she said. "And my mom and dad."

"This is great. Hell yes I'm running it. We've got a good paper coming up this week."

Serena pointed, "You got a good story out at the hog farm?"

"The owner's a good story. Interesting character. A braggart, but humorous and friendly. However I have a feeling he could turn on you in a second. He was glad to see me I think. He wants a copy of the article so I'm sticking the seven murders in there for him to read. And the guy who says he's suing the hog farm, though I can't verify he has actually filed suit since I can't get the records from the circuit clerk. The owner, Miehle, will either get back to me and raise hell about it or maybe I'll get some answers."

"You think he's behind all the murders?"

Cooper stopped typing, stared at his screen and said, "I don't know. He seems like one of the good ol' boys, but I didn't push him. Not the first time. Let's see what he says about my article."

"Ten more subscriptions today," Serena said.

"Hey, I want you to go over my article on the hog farm. See if I missed anything."

Serena was silent. She moved papers around on her desk, then looking at Cooper said, "You're the boss."

Graham gave the *Special Edition* a good print job, the front page picture of Ev Miehle and his sow with eight pigs came out sharp and crisp. The print came out with good contrast and no smears. Cooper held a copy at arms length and said to Serena, "We've got a paper this week, Kid."

Serena, peeling labels off the roll quickly and putting them on each paper, said without stopping her motion, "Twenty-five hundred twenty dollars in ads. Plus six hundred in sixty new subscriptions. Maybe we can raise the subscription price now that people actually want one. Ten dollars doesn't even pay the postage."

Cooper grabbed some papers and started helping her with the labels. "Sure. You're in charge of circulation aren't you?"

She laughed. "I need a nameplate for my desk with all my titles on it."

"You deserve a raise."

"After today's edition, so do you. Those new subscriptions aren't coming in because of anything I do."

A man came through the front door, saw the papers stacked up on the floor and said, "That this week's?"

Serena handed a copy to him, took his quarter while the man scanned the front of the paper. "Hmph," he said. "See you made it out to the perfume factory."

Others came in to get a copy of their hometown paper. Cooper took the labeled papers to the post office and came back to the office to close up for the day. Serena told him they had sold thirty papers that afternoon. "Maybe we ought to raise the single copy price while we're at it," she said. "And next week increase the print run by a hundred copies. I have a feeling we're going to be selling more papers."

"Or none if Ev Miehle doesn't like my story and shuts us down."

She had a full blown head of red, curly hair, could almost be called an afro if her skin hadn't been so white and translucent. She strode directly to Cooper's house-door table, slammed a newspaper down in front of him and said, "You Rease?"

He took his eyes off the monitor to take her in, her short stature, her flowing smock adorned with multi-colored flowers, her bushy hair and lastly her blazing, blue eyes.

"I'm Cooper Rease," he said. "And you are?"

"Carmello Stonebridge," she barked, her voice too large for such a small woman. She appeared maybe thirty, but difficult to tell, her skin so smooth and so white. "I read your glowing article about our fabulous community betterment." She hammered the table under the newspaper and jabbed a forefinger at the front page image of Ev Miehle. "Boy, did old Ev get to you. How much did he pay you for such a glorious write-up?"

"You a subscriber?" Cooper asked evenly.

"Well, I paid a quarter for the damn rag if that's what you're asking?"

"That entitles you to put in your two-bits worth."

"You know who the Miehle brothers are?" Without waiting for Cooper to answer, she told him. "They're the biggest bankroller in the country for the Nazi party. I notice you called it the Republican party. They own the Soldano Chemical works, the outfit that poisons all the seed farmers plant anymore because the farmers are too lazy to keep the weeds out of their crops."

"Big fan of farmers, I see," Cooper offered.

"Real farmers, yes. Welfare farmers, corporate farmers, no. Did you check on how the hog farm got a permit from the state Environmental Quality? You check on how Farm Services approved a low interest loan to build the farm? You check on anything or did you just accept the unbiased bullshit from good ol' boy Ev Miehle?"

"Why don't you tell me about it." Cooper, being calm despite the blast from the red-headed siren.

"Why don't you get off you butt and investigate it, big-time journalist. I checked up on you, you're all over the internet. Fired twice, went to jail. You did a good job on the timber cutters, but lost your job because of it. So, what's wrong now, afraid you'll get fired again so you just throw out a softball piece on the richest man in the state?"

Cooper's face burned. Anger rose in him like an out-of-control fire. He took two deep breaths—a lesson he had learned in prison—put a smile on his face, looked at the woman's mouth—another lesson he learned in prison, don't look at her eyes—and said, "What exactly is your interest in this?"

She flipped the newspaper over to page eight where Cooper had jumped the hog farm article from page one. The seven names of the unexplained deaths he had put in the story had all been highlighted with a yellow pen. Carmello Stonebridge jabbed at one name. "Elsie Loring," she snapped. "My mother. Murdered."

Cooper took a new look at her, this time her blazing eyes, how deep they were, like two blue lasers. He pointed at another highlighted name. "Cecilia Roth. My mother."

It was her turn to take a new look at him. Some of the fire in her eyes dimmed. Her mouth relaxed, the lips not so taut. In a lower voice she said, "Ah, so. Is that why you're here?"

"Yes," he said. "And you?"

She put her hand out across the house-door table and he took it, small and warm, but strong.

"I'm going to need your help," he said.

She took a card from her purse and handed it to him. "I'm late for an appointment. Call me."

As she was leaving out the door, he said, "I will."

He stared after her, watched her get into a Mercedes and drive away. He blew out a breath and looked at Serena.

"I should have warned you about her," she said.

Carmello Stonebridge had gotten to New Port four days after the last legal day to file with the probate judge as an heir. She brought Strefan Robensen, her lover—would have been her wife if it had been legal in the state—with her. Her mother's eight acres of property and the rest of her belongings including eleven thousand dollars had gone to the state, "According to the law," Judge Harold Turner told her.

The accident report on the incident in which Elsie Loring was killed, became lost somewhere in the shuffle. The Highway Patrol said the file had gone to the Cluster County Sheriff's office who had the jurisdiction for the accident which had occurred on a city street in New Port. Sheriff Walker Burnett first told her the report was in the hands of the Highway Patrol, then said his office was still investigating the case and the file was closed. That had been a year ago. She told this to Cooper in one, uninterrupted sentence when he called her that evening.

"How did her eight acres end up in the hog farm?" he asked.

"Damn good question. You need to start with the frigging judge and work your way up to Jack Stadler, the assessor. Of course, he won't tell you anything, but he's got to be in on it. Then go on out to Farm Services. Grady Quichen. He's a weasel. He's the one who gave the go ahead to the hog farm. That's where I met old Ev Miehle. Old Ev, he was "Plumb flabbergasted," how I was being treated. Asked weasel-faced Quichen couldn't he make an exception in my case and old weasel Quichen says, "Hell, Ev, I got to obey the law. Same as I did in your case."

"He said that?"Cooper asked.

"Exact words. Ask Strefan, she was there. And boy did they do some googling at her. Imagine that, a black woman and a red-headed white woman living together. I'll bet they're still talking about it down at the courthouse."

"And you filed suit against the county?"

"Frigging judge—what's his name? Harold. Good Old Boy Harold—threw it out. Four days late. Never mind they never made an effort to serve me with the papers like they're required to do. Mom never made a will, I was an only child, no other close relatives. Mom didn't exactly subscribe to my lifestyle, but she did have my name on a card in her purse to notify in case of accident. Sheriff says it wasn't on her, but I know better. They finally gave me her purse without the wallet. You know she wouldn't be driving around without a wallet and drivers license."

"So what's your next step?"

"File another lawsuit. We're both working at the hospital, Strefan's got her LPN and I'm a candy striper. Damn lawyer wants five thousand advance and thirty percent of any damages I collect from the county. Ha."

"How did you get involved with Environmental Quality and the hog farm?"

"Well, mostly from old Ev Miehle spouting off about how I should have been helped. But when the conversation got around to Mom's eight acres and the hog farm, I got shuffled aside. So, I'm thinking what the hell is a hog farm doing out there, anyway.

The Special Edition

You know the runoff is going to go into the springs a couple of miles down the road. The springs are part of a state park, aren't they? I mean, how could they okay all that pig shit running off into that clear spring that runs underground for miles and miles?"

"And what exactly have you found out?"

A long pause followed and Cooper could hear Carmello Stonebridge breathing into the phone.

"I guess I haven't found out a damn thing. I think the editor there before you might have found out something. I told her everything I've told you and a week later she said she got hold of the records and that Lou Steubbin—I think that's the name she told me—in the state water quality office had never seen the report done by EPA and that the only papers on file were the ones Farm Services did okaying a loan for the farm based on the state environmental agency's approval. Lots of bureaucratic bull shit, you ask me. Or, in this case, pig shit."

"You're talking about the woman named Allen?"

"Lisa Allen," Carmello Stonebridge said. "Yeah, that was her name. What happened to her?"\

"Don't know," Cooper said. "You never heard?"

"There's so damn many people in this county involved and she was starting to make up the list. Somebody got to her, I guess."

Cooper pulled a blank sheet of paper out of the printer stack, took a pen in hand and said, "Guess I'll start my own list. Who should I write down first?"

"Sheriff Walker Burnett," she said.

He wrote the name. "Stay in touch," he told her. He looked at Serena, busy at printing out ads, and told her, "I'll be at the courthouse."

She looked up from her computer screen. "Heard our sheriff's report on the radio this morning. The station in Cluster. At least they gave us credit for it, gave the name of the paper."

"Good advertisement for us. What else did they say?"

"They read the lead on the hog farm story."

"Yeah? I should be pissed off about providing news for their program, but maybe it'll get us a few more subscriptions."

"Two people came in this morning for subscriptions. Said they wanted to read about the hog farm."

"Good. What else have you accomplished so far today?"

Hands still on the keyboard, she said, "I sent you a couple of emails. We got another anonymous letter with more courthouse reports and Sheriff Walker Burnett called. He wants to see you in his office."

Cooper smiled and circled the only name on his list.

Sheriff Walker Burnett looked as if he had been sitting at his desk waiting for Cooper. Without speaking, he waved toward the one chair facing his desk.

"Coffee?" he asked.

"No, thanks," Cooper said, taking a seat in the worn, wooden Windsor chair. "I hear you wanted to see me."

"I need to know where you've been getting the information you printed in your paper from the incident report file that's closed to the public," the sheriff said in an even tone.

"Why are the reports closed?" Cooper asked.

"We investigate all the incidents our officers are called to investigate. The reports remain closed to the public until we have investigated them thoroughly."

"What about your file on the death of Grant Borden? Is that still under investigation?"

"There's no investigation in that death. The coroner's report says he died from a self inflicted gunshot."

"He was shot twice in the head. Were both of the shots self-inflicted?"

"You need to ask the coroner about that. It's in his report."

"And Magliolie? That still under investigation? Trying to discover who's shotgun he used to shoot himself? His wife says he never owned a shotgun"

Sheriff Burnett waved the question off with a hand, then sipped from his coffee cup. "Some men don't tell their wife everything."

"Cecilia Roth," Cooper said, trying to keep his voice even with the mention of his mother's name. "I guess you're still looking for the perpetrator."

"Something's bound to turn up," Burnett said. "Always does."

"So that file's closed also."

"We're not revealing any names from our investigation until it's settled. People could get the wrong idea. Just because we talked with someone about it doesn't mean that person's guilty."

"Elsie Loring? The woman who got run over inside the city limits of New Port?"

Burnett picked a frosted donut from a box that was under a copy of the *Special Edition*, shoved the box across the desk and motioned toward it for Cooper who waved it away. He bit into the donut and said while chewing with flakes of frosted icing dribbling from his mouth, "My office contracts with the city down there for protection. So, the reports on anything happens there belong to the city. You'll have to ask the mayor or the city council about that matter."

"Someone said you told them the Highway Patrol was investigating the case and the Highway Patrol said your office was."

Burnett finished the donut, licked his fingers and washed it down with a sip of coffee. He was still standing when he said, "You must be talking about that red-headed woman who's shacking up with the black girl. She's going to have to cut back on the loose talk she's been spreading around. She's accusing everybody of just about everything. And here she is breaking all the moral codes of society."

"You're not going to arrest her for sleeping with a black woman are you?"

Burnett didn't take it well. "Look," he said, placing his hands on the desk and looking down at Cooper, "you want to get along in this county it would do you well to stop listening to the people who came here trying to destroy everything."

"Our subscriptions are up dramatically since I printed the incident report. Radio picked it up, they liked it." Cooper couldn't prevent the half smile on his face.

"Hell yes, people like to read dirt, even when it's all lies. That the kind of newspaper you want to print, you won't last long. And you won't be hearing anymore crap that you print on that radio station, I guarantee."

"I see," Cooper said. "I don't suppose there's any use asking you about Jose Rodriquez, Walter Clipton or Martin Dinsmore since, I'm sure, all their files are closed or under investigation."

Walker Burnett straightened and his small potbelly stretched the button holes on his pressed and creased uniform blouse. He laughed for a moment before saying, "Yeah, I read your piece about the hog farm and how you threw all those people in the story as if they had any connection at all with that operation. But, hell, you left out the three teenagers who died in a car wreck last year out on the highway with all three of them full of meth and other dope. And you didn't put in the part about old man Simmons, ninety-one years old being found dead from a heart attack while trying to dig some post holes on his farm. Or the cook at the school who died on the floor in front of a couple hundred kid. You want, I could give you a list of people who died in the county the last four years."

"Okay," Cooper said. "Give me the list, I'll see how you investigated them."

"Ha," Burnett said. He walked around the desk and opened the door to his office and stood holding it for Cooper. "I'm a little busy right at the moment taking care of county business."

Cooper stood, turned deliberately toward the bank of gray metal filing cabinets, each row locked with a rod through the handles and a padlock at the top. "Just unlock the cabinets the files are in, I'll do the looking. No need to take up your valuable time."

"Not all those files are open to the public," Burnett said, looking firm.

"That's not in accordance with the state Freedom of Information Act."

"In my interpretation of the state statute, we're in full compliance."

Cooper said, "I guess we'll have to let a judge interpret the statute, then, Sheriff. Case law is pretty clear. There are penalties for public officials that refuse to comply."

"There are penalties for people who interfere with public

officials enforcing the laws of the state also," Burnett said.

"What kind of penalties?" Cooper asked.

The sheriff grew rigid, facing Cooper. "Boy, you break into my files again and publish stuff in your small time rag of a newspaper and you'll find out what happens to people who come into my town and defy the rules we've established."

"Are those rules published? Where would I find a list of your rules for your town?"

"I'll put it this way, you'll know when you've violated one of them. And you just did. I'm letting you off easy this one time. You publish closed files out of this office again and you'll be a guest of the county for thirty days."

"That sounds like a threat by a law enforcement officer." Cooper rose and walked to the door. Just before leaving he said, inches away from the sheriff still holding the door, "Next time you want to see me, you can come to my office. With a warrant."

Cooper came in and walked to Serena's all-metal desk. She looked up and he opened a spiral-wound notebook and showed her the empty pages.

"My reports from all the county officials."

"Planning on running more empty columns this week," she asked.

"No, by God." He retracted a small recorder from an inside jacket pocket, unclipped a miniature microphone from his jacket lapel and handed it to her. "How good are you at transcribing a recording?"

A line had formed at the door to the converted gas station when Serena rode up on her Triumph. She unlocked the door and let the dozen or so people inside where they quickly grabbed the latest copy of the *Special Edition* as Serena cut the ties on the bundles. As she took the money, she asked if anyone wanted to take out a subscription for only ten dollars. She took in ninety dollars in subscriptions and six dollars and fifty cents in single copy payments. When Cooper arrived she was still filling out subscriptions for the people inside.

A woman asked him, "When you going to do something about that damn hog farm out there and all them killin's?"

"We're working on it," he said. "We could use all the help we can get. What do you know about the kilings?"

"Hmmph," the woman said through her nose. "I know plenty. I know them people—that Roth woman and that Loring woman didn't get killed by no stranger. Ever body knows that."

"What I need is proof," Cooper said. Several other people, with newspaper in hand, stood listening to Cooper and the woman. One man, with the paper spread to the article written from Cooper's recording of the sheriff, said, "You better lock your doors at night. Old Sheriff Burnett, he's one mean son of a bitch."

Cooper asked the people around him, looking at them one by

one, if anyone had any information about the deaths that had occurred or about the establishment of the hog farm. Anything he could print. They looked away and edged toward the door. One woman said, "We're glad you're doing this." As she went out the door she added, "Watch your back."

Serena continued to sell copies and take subscriptions for the next hour. Cooper sat reading through the latest copy of the *Special Edition*, picking apart sentences he should have re-written and those where Serena had corrected grammar and punctuation. His weak suits. When at last the stream of readers abated, she looked at him.

"Whew," she said. "I think you hit a nerve in the community with that article about the sheriff."

"He promised retribution," Cooper said. "You checked on the incident reports this week I hope."

"Four of them verified."

She looked at her phone lying on her All-Metal desk. "Aha," she said. "Our first Tweet."

"What?" he asked. "What Tweet? What's a Tweet. How did we get on the Tweet network or whatever."

"I put us on," she said. "Have to be up to date. I'm adding a web site and Facebook."

"I don't know anything about those," Cooper said. "I've been kind of computer-limited the last couple of years."

"No computers in prison?"

"Yeah, but I was denied usage because they were afraid, me being a journalist, I might start writing editorials or something. What's the Tweet say?"

"It's from our courthouse spy. It says, "Don't reply. Full reports from every office this week. Check Grady Quichen taxes.""

The Special Edition

"So you've got the name or hash tag or whatever of the person who sent it?"

"Yeah."

"Delete it," Cooper told her. "Go through both our computers and delete anything that would implicate anyone other than the newspaper. Don't be surprised if the sheriff or his deputies come in and confiscate our computers and our files. If they do, call me, but don't resist or they'll throw you in jail."

"Do you expect them to do that?" A bit of a scared look ran across her face, but was quickly replaced by a stern look of resistance. "Okay if I kick them in the shins?"

He grinned. "Make sure they give you a receipt for everything they take and make sure they show you a warrant."

"Where will you be?"

"At the courthouse looking at tax records."

The fallout from the latest edition of the newspaper started when he walked into the office for county records.

"Computer's are down," the records clerk said. "Sorry."

"So I won't be able to check on properties in the county and their tax records?" Cooper asked.

"You can check back, but I don't know how long we'll be down. It's sporadic."

"You mean, when I walk in the door it goes down?"

She smiled and swept back a styled, brushed and sprayed roll of not quite brown, not quite amber hair behind one ear decorated with a dangling sparkle of jewels. Mary Giles was maybe fifty with an almost square physique that looked restrained under a colorful dress with large flowers in various colors. Her smile spreading across her entire countenance was artificial and pompous.

"I wonder if the assessor's computer is also down," Cooper said as he left.

Inside the assessor's office the clerk told him that Mister Stadler, the assessor, was not in the office. Cooper looked at the half-opened door with Stadler's name on it and saw an older man, white hair, hard jaw, sitting at a rolltop desk looking over some papers.

"When do you expect him?" Cooper asked.

"He didn't say," the woman told him. She looked straight at him, no smile, no expression, as if she expected to be challenged. She was young, probably still in her twenties and a bit too much of a barroom look to her to be called attractive.

Cooper flashed her a "I know what you're up to," crooked grin and said, "Maybe I'll just wait for him. He might decide to come out. Or come back. Whatever."

She turned away from him and went through the half-opened door, closing it behind her. Cooper sat in one of three straight, hard chairs across from her desk. He kept an eye on the old, school-type clock on the wall of the outside office and for ten minutes the door never opened and no one came out. His cell rang. Serena said, "Sheriff Walker Burnett is here with a warrant for your arrest and a warrant for our computers and our phones."

"What am I being arrested for?"

"Something like inciting a riot, couldn't read it fast enough."

"Can he hear you?"

"No, I'm in the restroom flushing the toilet."

"Stay in the restroom and lock the door until they leave. Then lock the office and go home until you hear from me."

The Special Edition

A long pause while Cooper listened to the toilet flushing on the other end. Then, "I know a lawyer."

"So do I," he said. "Mine's better. The attorney general."

Cooper Rease had gone to school at the university with Taylor Stephens. While Cooper had floundered around messing up his life, Taylor had become quite successful in his father's law firm. And after his father was elected attorney general for the state, Taylor rose in the ranks of the law firm. He had been the acting attorney for Cooper and for the *Kansas City Star* when Cooper had been sentenced. He told Cooper he could have gotten him off if he hadn't punched the prosecutor. *The Star* had told him the same thing.

At first, Taylor wasn't in, then when the receptionist came back on the phone, after Cooper gave her his name, she said, "One moment for Mister Stephens."

"Dammit, Cooper," said a familiar voice, "what the hell are you into now?"

"My First Amendment rights have been violated," Cooper said. "And hello to you, too, Mister Big Shot."

Taylor Stephens laughed. "Again? My god, you wear those First Amendment rights on your sleeve. Tell me about it. And if you go punching anymore elected officials we never had this conversation."

Cooper related his predicament, trying to be brief, but he was finding it difficult finding a place to stop. When he halted for breath, Taylor interrupted. "Okay, I get it. I've got Maria contacting Winslow—he does the federal stuff around here, you know like civil rights, all that. He was on the case of yours before if you remember. He'll file an injunction that'll have that half-assed sheriff up there kissing your butt before the day is over. Just don't do anything crazy. You could follow up with a civil case if you want, but that gets expensive and drawn out when you go against an elected official because the county is bound to have all kinds of ordinances we would have to have declared unconstitutional. You probably don't want to go that way."

"Taylor, I'm broke. How am I going to pay you for all this?"

"You might start by paying me back for all the beer I bought you in school. Besides, remember I told you journalism didn't pay worth a damn."

"You were right about that."

"All right. I'm carrying you on the cuff. Someday I'm coming up there to collect. They sell double malted scotch up there don't they?"

"Never heard of it. Settle for some home brew?"

Taylor laughed. "Let me know how all this turns out. Call Winslow if you need anything else."

"A good friend is all I need," Cooper said. "And I've got one."

At four o'clock that afternoon a U.S. Marshal delivered an injunction in the Cluster County courthouse directing Sheriff Walker Burnett to return all property seized from the newspaper and to quash all warrants against Cooper Rease and anyone else affiliated with the newspaper. In addition, Sheriff Burnett was personally served with seven counts against him for violating civil rights and constitutional rights of Cooper Rease. At five o'clock Sheriff Burnett handed a letter of resignation to the Cluster County Commission.

At six o'clock Serena received another Tweet from Cluster-Mole telling her that Sheriff Burnett was no longer sheriff. Deputy Johnny Klemm, newly appointed sheriff by the commission appeared at the door to the gas station-office at six fifteen with the computers and her personal cell phone.

Serena closed the office at six-thirty and rode her Triumph directly to Cooper's mobile home where he sat drinking a beer and going over what information he had obtained from the county collector's office which, miraculously had seen their computers alive following the marshal's visit to the courthouse.

"Look at this," he told her after uncapping a Dr. Pepper for her. "Quichen had a million and a half valued personal and real property last year and paid no county taxes. It looks like the old guy, Stadler in the assessor's office is the one handing out local favors. He declared no taxes against Quichen, the Farm Services Agent for Cluster County, because he didn't pay federal income taxes. Now why wouldn't Quichen have to pay federal income taxes?"

"Why don't you ask him?"

"Yeah, right. Trouble is, he's not covered by the state freedom of information act. The federal act, yeah, but that takes time."

"I've got time."

"Okay." He opened another beer. "Okay, then. You can get to work on it tomorrow on your computer. Did they take anything off of it?

"I don't know, I haven't looked. I had copied everything off mine and yours—hope you don't mind—to my laptop. I had it in the restroom with me."

"They didn't break down the door?"

"I pretended I was calling nine-one-one and they could hear me say I was being raped. They left pretty quick."

He couldn't keep the smile off his face. "You're remarkably resourceful, you know it?"

"What do you think is going to happen next?"

At seven fifteen they heard the explosion that destroyed the gas-station office.

Hard copies of everything had gone up in flames. Cooper and Serena watched an incredibly inept fire department try to unroll tangled hoses that leaked more onto the street than came out the end of the hose. Neither of them spoke. Their thoughts were not on the records that were gone, but on the threats against them that were explicit in the burning rubble of the old station.

"I was growing kind of fond of the old joint," Cooper said.

"Was it a message or were they trying to kill us?"

Cooper saw what could be a sign of fear in her face. A wave of guilt rushed through him. Why hadn't he put it together? What was happening wasn't just harassment, obfuscation and simple hiding secrets in the county offices. What was happening were threats by people who had already committed seven murders. He put an arm around her and pulled her against him. She lay soft and warm against his side as she brushed a wave from her face.

"Goddam them," she said, her voice breaking. "We're going to bury those sons of bitches. They picked on the wrong people this time."

"Look," he said, "this is getting on the verge of being dangerous. I don't want you to be in the center of something I started."

She jabbed an elbow into his ribs. "Don't be trying to get rid of me. You can't fire me. I'm not quitting. I'm going to see that the bastards who caused all this pay for it."

Cooper saw Graham coming toward them past the outdated fire engines and the volunteers still fighting the useless hoses.

"Here comes the boss," he said. He took his arm from around Serena's shoulders and walked to meet Graham, who, seeing him coming toward him, stopped and watched the few remaining flames still alive in the rubble.

"Letter to the editor," Graham said. "Looks like someone took exception to your last edition."

"Cowards," Cooper said.

"Probably. Had a visitor today. Man owns three grocery stores in the county. Runs a double truck every week, four pages once a month. Suggested this paper ought to be closed down."

"So he came down here with a stick of dynamite. How does this paper hurt the three grocery stores?"

"He decides who runs for office in the courthouse."

"Was he the one who forced Burnett out?"

"He doesn't actually make any decisions. He either says yes or no."

"What's this guy's name?" Cooper asked.

"Tom Heard. Arrowhead Supermarkets."

"Arrowhead huh? Like in Arrowhead truck lines?"

Graham turned to look at him. "If you think you have it all figured out, you're wrong."

"Keep reading the *Special Edition*," Cooper said. "You'll find out."

Graham rubbed a hand across his face. "Look, the paper's your's if you can come up with twenty-five thousand dollars by Friday. Otherwise, you've printed the last *Special Edition*."

"You're giving in to the cowards?"

"I'm cutting my losses."

Cooper fought the anger he felt. "You're joining the cowards. Well, I'm not. They're going to have to kill me to stop me."

"Goddammit, don't you understand?" Graham snapped. "Go on back to wherever you came from. But if you want to commit suicide, keep on throwing salt in their eyes. I'm giving you the opportunity."

He walked away, got to ten feet before he stopped and turned back. "Friday," he said. "Twenty-five thousand."

12

The voice was familiar, though Cooper hadn't heard it for some years.

"Hello, Brother," Cooper said.

A long silence, then, "Well, well. Finally remembered the rest of your family."

"I've never forgotten you, Clay. I hope that goes both ways."

"How could I forget. You continue to make headlines. As does our father, who apparently has forgotten. Missed you at our mother's funeral."

"I was a bit indisposed, Clay."

"Yeah, I know. In the hoosegow wasn't it?"

"A small misunderstanding."

Clay laughed. "What could possibly move you to call your brother on this date?"

"Two things: one, I'm in New Port now. Where Mom was killed. I just bought the newspaper here and I'm working on the story about her murder and six others. So, I thought you could give me some information that might help."

"You showed a great lack of interest in her welfare. What's the reason for the big spurt of family love all of a sudden?"

"Maybe it's guilt, I don't know. When I was twelve I told her I hated her. I'm still paying for that."

Clay cleared his throat and Cooper waited.

The Special Edition

After the pause Clay said, "What do you want to know?" he asked.

"Everything you know about how she lived here. Who she knew. Where she got her money to live on. Did Dad send her any money? Did she have a job? Who were her friends?"

"I don't know all that. She was pretty tight mouthed about things like that. After I got out of the community college—could have been the university like you went to except our dear father never sent me any money—I've been out here in Colorado. She never asked me for money, I don't know where she got her money. She bought the place there from the money when she sold the house. That was my school money, too. Nothing came from dear old Dad who was galavanting all over the world killing people, apparently."

"Just to set it straight, our father never gave me any money for school, either. I worked my way through at the newspaper. Did Mom have a job here?"

"If she did she never told me about it. She did tell me the banker in town loaned her money on the place, which I guess he did. She had a mortgage so he got the property after she died. Seems she had equity of about ten thousand dollars that I ended up with about half of it after probate."

"She wasn't old enough for social security and if Dad didn't send her any money, she must have had some source of income."

Clay didn't answer for a while. Cooper thought for a moment he had hung up and when he said Clay's name, Clay said, "I sent her some money, not much. The only thing I ever heard her say about money was some people were always paying her for going through the caves. Like it was a tourist attraction."

"Caves?" Cooper said. "She had caves on her property?"

"Way I understand it, there are caves all over that part of the county. Only a few of them were accessible and her place was one of them. Why do people want to crawl around in caves?"

"Listen," Cooper halted, searching for the right words, "I'm trying to buy the newspaper here. I have to raise twenty-five thousand dollars. I thought maybe you would like to join with me trying to find out who killed our mother."

Clay laughed again, longer and louder this time. "I thought as much. You called me for money. Why wouldn't I guess that?"

"You would like to know who killed her, wouldn't you?"

"I've talked with the police there. They can't solve it, what makes you think you can."

"Because I care more than they do."

"And you think I don't care."

"I was hoping you would," 'Cooper said.

Clay said, scornful, a tone of sarcasm in his voice, "I invest in your newspaper and the next thing I know, you're in jail again or somebody's suing you. I don't think I want to be involved, Cooper. Call me when you find out who killed our mother."

The line went dead.

J.S. Larkin, President, the plaque on the office wall read. Cooper stood in the aisle until a stylishly dressed young woman approached and asked if she could help.

"My name is Cooper Rease. I'd like to talk with Mister Larkin about a loan."

"Oh, that would be Mister Grant. He's the one who does our loan approvals."

The Special Edition

"Mister Larkin had spoken with Cecilia Roth about a loan he had taken out for her on her property. That particular loan has a bearing on my application."

"Mmm," the woman mused, delaying and a bit confused about how to handle his request. She looked at the man seated inside the office with Larkin's name on it. He was a tall, rather thin man with a mass of white hair and a slender, well clipped mustache. She walked through the door to his desk, waited until she was acknowledged, then spoke to him. The man looked at Cooper, then spoke one word to the young woman. She came back to Cooper and said, "Mister Larkin will see you now."

Cooper walked to the front of the desk and when the man looked up at him, Cooper stuck his hand across the desk and gave his name. Larkin gripped his hand and waved to a cushioned chair fronting the desk.

"You mentioned Mrs. Cecilia Roth, I believe," Larkin said, a statement not a question.

"I'm her son," Cooper said.

"Ahh," Larkin nodded. "My condolences. A terrible crime. She was a pleasant woman. Our relationship was mutually re-spective."

"I understand you held a mortgage on her ten acres," Cooper said.

"Yes, we did. I believe we sent a check to you for the equity she had in the property."

"You sold the property to The State Bank of Kansas City, I understand."

"That's correct," Larkin said. "I believe we gave you the de-tails. She was a bit in arrears in payments. And I think some of the probate costs were subtracted."

"So, I assume, you were the agent in the sale of the Elsie Loring farm to the same bank."

Larkin stiffened in his chair and ran one hand across the slim, white mustache. "That had no connection to your mother's property."

"And the Dinsmore farm? And Grant Borden's farm? You were the agent in the sale of all of those farms to the Kansas City bank?"

Larkin's friendly demeanor had undergone a one-hundred-eighty degree change. "Afraid I don't understand. I was told you wanted to discuss a loan and how it was related to your mother's property."

"I am the son of Cecilia Roth. But not the son who collected the five thousand dollars of the ten thousand dollar equity in her property. That would be my brother Clay. I'm Cooper Rease. I'm the editor of the newspaper here in town. The one you advertise in. *The Special Edition*."

Larkin's lips barely moved when he said, "You're here for an article in the newspaper?"

"Well, yeah," Cooper said. "That and I wanted to tell you I'm buying the newspaper from Mister Graham. I need a loan of twenty-five thousand dollars."

Larkin's interest now was invested in items on his desktop as he shuffled papers into different locations. Reproachfully, he leaned both forearms on the desk and with narrowed eyes said, "Am I mistaken in assuming you are saying if the bank grants you a loan of twenty-five thousand dollars you won't write an article implying the bank was involved with the killing of the owners of those properties?"

Cooper was taken aback by Larkin's remark. "If I gave that

impression then I apologize. I can see where you might have reason to think that. I can assure you that my newspaper will make no such accusation or implication of any kind against you or anyone without facts. I want to find out who and why my mother and those other six people were murdered. And I intend to do that. I would like to conduct all my business here in New Port. I can get a loan with some out of town institution but I would prefer it was here."

"I think it would not be wise for the bank to be involved in the operation of the newspaper," Larkin said. He picked up the telephone on his desk, looked directly at Cooper and said, "Now if you'll excuse me."

Cooper rose. "Thanks for your time, Mr. Larkin. I talked with Ev Miehle. I checked the stockholders of your bank. He and his brother own controlling interest in the Home Bank of New Port I notice. Same as the Soldano hog farm."

13

Serena was at the small kitchen table inside his mobile home working on her computer. She sat on a stack of books to be the proper height for keyboard work. He'd told her to stay there the morning after the fire took the gas station office and she had come on her Triumph.

"Maybe we should put a sign up outside," she said. "If this is the new office of the *Special Edition* we need to let people know where to come for the paper."

Cooper flopped down in the wobbly recliner. "We can't call it the *Special Edition* anymore."

"Why?"

"You know, I told you that Graham wants twenty-five thousand for the paper or he's closing it down. So, I'm going to have to start my own paper. I don't have twenty-five thousand and the bank won't loan it to me."

"Why not?"

"Because I was stupid. I went in asking about how the bank sold my mother's property and those other people's who were murdered. Made it sound like I was accusing them. The banker took offense and declined to invest in the paper."

"What should I tell the advertisers?"

"I don't know. I've got to think this through. I can't pay you anything and nobody's going to advertise with a start-up newspaper. And I can't afford to print it and mail it because it takes two years to get a second class postage permit and I can't afford bulk mail. And an online paper won't pay enough to feed me let alone pay your salary."

She said, "Graham had the place insured for a hundred thousand dollars."

Cooper said, "What? Are you sure? How did you know?"

"Met the insurance guy out at the old station this morning. He assumed I knew it was insured. Fire marshal was there, too. Said dynamite was used to blow the station up."

"Damn," Cooper said and walked to the refrigerator in need of a beer.

Serena said, "I made coffee."

He stopped with his hand on the door handle. He looked at her and she looked back at him. "Okay," he said and went to the coffee pot and filled a cup.

"I overheard the fire marshal say to our new sheriff that Grant Borden's house had been dynamited, also."

"Interesting," Cooper said. "You even snoop well."

"Got another Tweet," she said. He looked at her. "Said to check Edward Bilbo."

"The used car dealer?" Cooper asked. "Who was that from?"

"ListenUp was the tag."

He drank from the cup and waited for her to go on.

"That was the name of the other editor's column," she said. "Lisa Allen's Listen Up."

Cooper thought about it. "The woman who was the editor before me? Interesting. Wonder what she meant about the used car dealer."

"I Googled Edward Bilbo, did a background check. What I

found out was that he has a record. One you'll want to hear."

"Yeah? What's he done?"

"Spent two years in the penitentiary for blowing up a car repair shop in South Missouri."

"Dynamite?"

"Would be my guess."

"I'll be damned," Cooper said, taking another drink of coffee not strong enough for him, but he wasn't going to tell her that. "Why would Bilbo blow up the newspaper office? You didn't piss him off when you sold him an ad did you?"

"Quite the opposite. He thought some kind of personal favor might be worked out for the price of an ad. I might have given him some reason for being encouraged. Not anything to take it out on the newspaper, though."

"If Graham hadn't pulled the paper out from under us I guess I would have to go talk with this Bilbo. Since I'm not the editor any longer I guess I don't care why he blew up the office."

"I've got one more thing for you," Serena said. She got up from the stack of books and walked over to his recliner. She handed him a slip of paper. With a question on his face, he took the paper and looked at it. A check for twenty-five thousand dollars.

She walked back to the table and pulled herself up on the stack of books and started tapping the keyboard. He sat speechless, staring at the check in his hand.

"Let's get to work, boss. We've got a paper to get out," she said.

Fernando and Rosalind Gonzalez both welcomed Cooper at the door to their modest home. Serena placed a hand on his back urging him inside. She introduced her parents to him, calling him, "Cooper, the boss." Followed by a short sentence in Spanish that he thought meant that he was an all-right person.

Both the parents, short and dark, greeted him amicably. His first impression was how much Serena was like her parents, courteous, serious and polite. Her mother asked if he would like a cold glass of lemonade and he said that he would enjoy one very much. Serena guided him to a leather recliner far more comfortable than the one in his rented mobile home. When Rosalind returned with his cool glass of lemonade and took a seat on the sofa facing him, Serena sat in the other recliner angled to face both him and her parents.

Cooper took a drink of the lemonade—well made and tasty with a sprig of mint floating on the surface—and thanked Rosalind. Though he felt uncomfortable, because of the purpose of his visit, neither the parents nor Serena seemed to be.

"Serena gave me the check," he said. "I'm at a loss on what to say. She says you have a very successful business here and you obviously work hard keeping it that way. That's why I'm reluctant to accept the loan. While you have worked so hard and put in so many long hours over the last ten or twelve years since you have been here, I have not been that good of a citizen."

He took another drink. "That's why I find it difficult to accept the check. I don't deserve it."

Fernando smiled slightly. "Serena thinks you do. She says you are the person this town needs. That the newspaper will drive the crime out of the town, out of the county. That only you can do it."

Cooper looked at Serena who sat relaxed in the recliner smiling back at him.

"Your daughter has done more than I have," he said. "She's an exceptional person."

"That is true," Rosalind said. "But she says you have the experience she lacks." Then she added, "And, she's a woman."

"I couldn't be sure I would ever be able to pay you back," Cooper said.

"That's why the loan," Serena said. "To guarantee you won't run out on us."

He glanced quickly at her and saw her still smiling.

"But it's your parents' money," he said. "That makes you the owner of the paper."

She shook her head. "I gather the information, you know what to do with it. Besides, I'm not sure I want to be a newspaper owner. I don't know what I want to do in life, yet. I want some time to decide."

"But, it's your money," Cooper said, pleading with the parents. "I know you've done well to save that much money, but what if I fail you. I've failed a lot of people including my mother. What if you lose the money."

"What will our business be worth if the things that are happening in this community aren't stopped," Fernando said.

The Special Edition

"Twenty-five thousand dollars is a very small amount of money to turn this community back into the place it was when we came here. The taxes on our property have doubled each year for the last three years. There is a man in Cluster who owns three grocery stores. He's buying the grocery store here. He doesn't want us in business. We've had three safety inspections in the last year. Once they forced us to destroy perfectly good produce because the inspector said it was rotten. I expect any day for the authorities to tell us we have to close our business. Twenty-five thousand dollars is a very small investment to put a stop to the people who are in charge in this county."

Cooper breathed heavily, at a loss for words. Serena rose from the recliner and said, "Let's get back to work, boss. Time's a wasting and we've got a paper to get out."

Graham didn't want to see him. Cooper was sure Graham didn't think he could possibly raise the money in New Port to buy the paper. He heard the woman in the front office tell Graham Cooper Rease was here to see him and he heard Graham say, "Damn."

The woman waved Cooper into Graham's office, left through the door and closed it behind her. Graham put down his pen and turned to Cooper. Taking the check from his pocket, Cooper laid it on Graham's desk and said, "There's your money, now let's sign the papers."

Graham looked at the check. "Fifteen thousand. You're ten thousand short."

"Take it out of the hundred thousand insurance money. The personal items I lost in the explosion were worth ten thousand."

"That's a lot of personal items," Graham said.

"That's a lot of insurance on a seventy year old gas station about to fall in."

Graham extended the check toward Cooper. "Afraid this won't do."

Cooper ignored the check. "How about I have a talk with the fire marshal. Not the local yokel, the one at the capital. I talked with the new sheriff, Good Ol' Boy Johnny Klemm. He's not interested in investigating the explosion, dynamite or no dynamite. Fire marshal won't swear it was dynamite. Sheriff Johnny says the owner—that would be you—declines to file any charges. Now, how close are you and the used car dealer, Bilbo. He's got a record of using dynamite. Grant Borden's fire resulted from dynamite. So let's have a conversation with the authorities in the capital, bypassing the local boys, and let's see how deeply you are involved with all those incidents."

Graham let his hand holding the check drop onto the desktop. "Dammit," he said, "I should have known better than hire you in the first place. You got no idea what the hell you're getting into."

"If you know, why aren't you saying so. You're the guardian of the truth, the fifth estate. Why the hell isn't your paper doing what I'm trying to do?"

Graham expressed exasperation. "Look," he said, "they took it all, everything I had. Had a five hundred forty acre farm. It's part of the hog farm, now. I'm listed as the publisher of the paper here, but I don't own it. Not anymore. I need a hundred thousand dollars to get my son out of prison. I scraped up everything I had and came up twenty-five thousand short. The hundred thousand insurance? Insurance company is rejecting it because it was an explosion. They may pay off eventually, but I can't wait."

"Did you have Bilbo blow the place up?"

"Hell no. How would I know somebody wasn't in the building? Think I wanted to kill somebody?"

"Why did he blow it up, then?"

"Hell, I don't know. You're starting to get somebody pissed off at you. Besides, they don't know I own the *Special Edition*."

"You keep saying they. Who are you talking about?"

Graham stared hard at Cooper. "All of them. Everybody in the courthouse. Soldano. State environmental, Farm Services. But I got no proof of any of that. I just know, that's all."

Cooper said, "How did they get your farm and your business? I don't understand why you let them take it."

"All I'm going to tell you is that my son got into things he shouldn't have and I took a step to help him. Trouble is, once you take that step, you just keep getting in deeper and deeper. I'm hoping this is the last step. Hell, it'll have to be. I got nothing else to sell. I need the twenty-five, not fifteen. I know a man in Minnesota who'll give me twenty-five for it. He's a shark. He gets his hook into the county he'll run the paper here out of business, but why do I care about that. I don't own controlling interest."

"Who does?"

"The bank. The bank owns everything. Soldano owns the bank."

Cooper took out his new check book he had just gotten from the bank when he deposited the check from the Gonzalez. "All right, I'll write you another check, but from now on, you're on my side. You tell me what you know and whatever you find out."

Graham said simply, "Thank you." Then followed with, "I still wish to hell I'd never hired you."

15

"Listen up," Serena said, looking at her Smart Phone. Cooper waited, but she said no more until she laid the phone aside and glanced at him sitting on the nearly-collapsed bar stool before his well worn kitchen counter littered with peanut shells. He crunched another peanut shell, popped the unsheathed nuts into his mouth and chewed away as she watched.

"It's her," she said. "The old editor."

"What's she saying?" he asked and crunched another shell.

"Card's stretch time."

He chewed, drank from the bottle of Boulevard Wheat Pilsner and said, "What's that mean?"

She shrugged.

"Cards?" he asked. "With an apostrophe?"

She looked. "Yes."

"Stretch not stitch?"

"Yes."

"Cards could be the baseball team. St. Louis Cardinals."

"She shrugged again. "I don't play baseball."

"Pity. You'd make a great shortstop."

She dead-panned him. "Is that supposed to be funny?"

"Come on, Serena, loosen up."

"So what does a baseball team have to do with Soldano and the hog farm. Or with seven murders?"

"Stretch time is the seventh inning. Seven murders."

"She can add."

He shelled another peanut and held the two shiny, peeled nuts out to her. She took them and chewed and waited. He popped a couple more bared nuts into his mouth, devoured them and said, "I think she means when the Cardinals are in the seventh inning she's going to call us."

"So we're going to watch baseball tonight?"

"That's a good idea. Wish I had a TV."

She picked up her Smart Phone. "What channel?"

He told her, she slid across the screen, tapped and held it out to him. He looked at the picture of the baseball game, picked up her phone, looked closer and said, "It's the sixth inning."

"How do you know she will call us?"

"I'm guessing." They both sat silently, Cooper crunching peanuts, Serena pecking her keyboard and watching the screen. He finished the beer, went to the refrigerator, got another, asked if she wanted a Dr. Pepper. She declined. Minutes later he announced, "Seventh inning."

A knock sounded at the door.

16

Lisa Allen was svelte, blonde, long limbed, tanned and appeared a bit anxious. Cooper said, "Hello Lisa."

"You got my message," she said.

"Please come in to our new office." He stepped aside and waved her inside. She looked around as if she expected someone to be watching her, took a few tenuous steps inside, saw Serena and stopped. "Who's she?" she asked.

"That's my staff. Serena, meet Lisa."

"Listen up," Serena said

Lisa Allen came into the room and stood, looking around. Cooper closed the door and offered the recliner to Lisa. She remained standing.

"I see you got rid of Burnett," she said. "He's an asshole. Fits right in with the rest of them, though."

"We've been wanting to talk with you," Cooper said. "See what you know about the murders, the hog farm, the whole situation."

"My advice," she said, still looking Serena over, "get the hell out of town."

'Yeah, tell me about that," Cooper said. "Why did you run out. Left old Graham high and dry."

"Graham's all right. Scared to death. Cut every story I wrote about," (quote marks with her fingers,) "the situation."

"What's he scared of?" Cooper asked.

"Same thing everyone in this stinking town is scared of. Being number eight."

"Told me he had problems with his son. Told me they, whoever they are, cleaned him out trying to help his son."

"The son's out in California. He's got real problems. Got in with a drug ring from Mexico. A bunch of people got killed, the Mexicans went back south of the border and Graham's son was left to face the music. No death penalty out there. Anywhere else like here in this state, his son would be executed.."

"Graham sold the paper to me," Cooper said. "Wanted money to get his son out of prison."

Lisa Allen laughed one short burst. "Sucker. Both of you. Whatever you paid for this paper you'll never get back. It's a loser. Graham isn't going to get his son out of prison. Fact is, they'll kill him in there. He knows too much."

"The big question is," Cooper said, "what do you know."

"I can't stay long enough to tell you everything I know. I checked on Bilbo and Wicker and they're both gone for the weekend. Jurgen is with his daddy in Europe. So I came back to get something that belongs to me. Then I'm gone."

"Who's Wicker? And who's Jurgen?"

Lisa laughed one short laugh again. "Boy, you don't know anything about what's going on here, do you? Bilbo sells stolen cars in his used car lot, didn't you know that? And his buddy Cody Wicker, the private eye, is who you hire if you want something done here, like kill somebody to get their land, that sort of thing. Jurgen? You never met him yet? That's old Ev Miehle's son."

"Hard jawed guy always needing a shave?"

"Sounds like Jurgen."

"What's Jurgen do?"

"Whatever Ev or Soldano wants done. He tells Bilbo, Bilbo tells Wicker and it gets done."

"So you think Wicker killed these seven people?" Cooper asked.

Lisa Allen watched Serena banging away on her computer. "Is she taking all this down?"

Cooper looked at Serena who's hands were now still. "What's wrong with that?" he asked.

"She puts my name in there and I'm dead."

He looked at Serena. "We don't reveal our sources," he said. "What we need is proof."

Again the short laugh. "I know you're a pro. *Kansas City Star*, all that. Professional journalist. They're pros too. You don't have billions of dollars at risk. They do. That makes them better pros than you. You are never going to hang any of this on Soldano. Good for you on the courthouse creeps, I don't know how you're getting into their files. You got Burnett, you can get the rest of the crowd at the courthouse. If that's what you want to do, you can do it. They're a bunch of losers and small time crooks taking money on the side, closing all their files. Even they don't know what they're involved in. But if you think you can tie their small time corruption to the big guys, I hate to disappoint you."

Cooper went to the refrigerator, took out two beers and a Dr. Pepper. He distributed them—Serena setting the Dr. Pepper beside her computer, Lisa Allen twisting the top off her beer and taking a drink—then he said to Lisa, conviction in his voice, "You're wrong. I'm going to find out who killed all those people and I'm going to put it in the *Special Edition* and I'm going to see them pay for it."

Lisa took another drink. "Let me tell you why I came back.

There was a Canon EOS camera here. Should have been here when you came. I want the memory card out of it."

Cooper went to the small table in the kitchen, picked up the Canon camera he had been using. He handed it to her. "This it?"

She took it. "Have you changed the memory card?"

"No."

"Looked at it?"

"Yes."

"Figures," she said. She pushed buttons and started watching a video. "That's Jurgen," she said, still watching.

"I wondered about that," Cooper said. "He's quite a big boy."

"Yes he is," Lisa said. She extracted the memory card and stuck it in her small shoulder hanging purse. "Hate for the wrong crowd to see this."

"Don't blame you."

She looked around again. "I lived here for a couple of weeks. A dump, you don't mind my saying so." She focused her eyes on Serena and said, "I'll tell you everything I know, which isn't much and it's not going to help you. I have to leave at four in the morning. Is she staying here tonight? There's only one bed."

Serena said, "Going to shoot another video?"

Cooper sat in the old, metal motel chair under the tree just outside the mobile home. He drank his coffee, watched the early morning sun lighting a string of soft white clouds chasing each other west to east. He was bothered by Lisa Allen's appearance. She had talked into the night as she removed piece by piece of clothing until wearing everything worn in the video she had taken with her: nothing.

Things were awkward after that. Resisting a sexy blonde as she beckoned him into bed with her was something he would have said he was not capable of. He drank too many beers, he listened to her talk about her escapades with Jurgen in the caves, in the gas station office, here in the mobile home and lastly, in the Super 8 on the highway. And he watched as she put the clothes back on and he listened as she told him how queer he was and finally, out of beer and out of naked blondes, he put on a pot of coffee and went outside to contemplate what had just taken place.

How was he going to explain the night to Serena. And why did he feel the need to? Lisa Allen had not known much that they could use. But he was interested in what she said about the caves, how Jurgen said the caves were why Soldano wanted Cooper's mother's land. Clay had said their mother talked about the caves on her property and how she charged money to let people explore them. What was it about the caves that Soldano wanted? He needed to explore those caves on his mother's ten acres.

Cooper thought the reason Lisa Allen had wanted the sex video of her and Jurgen Miehle wasn't to keep others from watching it, but because *she* wanted to watch it. He began running thoughts through his mind on how he might use her fascination for Jurgen to Cooper's advantage.

His thoughts then went to what she said about Soldano, that he would never be able to tie the murders back to them. He would visit Bilbo and Wicker see if he concurred with Lisa Allen's conclusion that it was the two of them who had killed Cecilia Roth and committed the other seven murders. He had to decide then what he would do if he was sure the two of them had been the ones who had killed his mother. Would he continue to publish the newspaper? Wasn't the real reason he came here was to find her killer? Why then, if he found him—or them—and he did something about it, would it be in his interest to continue his vow to end the corruption in the county and to pay Soldano back for his mother's murder? Where would it stop? Even if it was Bilbo and this guy, Wicker, wouldn't it have been Soldano who had ordered the murders? And did he now owe something more to the Gonzalez family?

Well, he owed them twenty-five thousand dollars, don't forget about that. How the hell was he going to repay them?

He began making further plans: go to Soldano's headquarters, talk with Carmello Stonebridge again, trace the granting of the permit for the hog farm. So many loose strings, how was he going to be able to tie them all together.

The town of New Port was strangely quiet this morning. Song birds' trilling echoed through the woods around the mobile home uninterrupted by normal sounds of civilization. Then he heard the purr of a motorcycle and that brought an expectation to him he was unable to explain. The sound drew closer and he watched Serena ride up to the mobile home and shut down the engine on the Triumph. Without looking at him she dismounted, took off her helmet and hung it on the handlebar, took her computer from the side bag and walked toward the mobile home. Just before opening the door she looked at him and said, "Your blonde guest take her sex tape and leave?"

An awkwardness had settled over the inside of the mobile home. Serena worked on the ads she had brought in with her. Cooper entered the story about a silo explosion close to town and what the volunteer fire chief had said about it. He realized then he did not have back copies of the newspaper, having lost them in the fire, so he called the fire chief and asked if there had been other silo fires in the county. The answer: No.

He stopped with his hands on the computer, looked at Serena and said, "You know that fifteen year old boy you told me about?"

Her hands stopped movement and she stared at her screen.

"Last night," he said, "I was him."

She tried to hide a smile with her hand before continuing on her work. "Whatever happened to that boy?" he asked.

She stopped again, said, "He came home last month from Afghanistan." Pause, then: "In a flag draped coffin." Looking at Cooper she said, "And that was the last time *I* ever cried."

He was silent for a while before saying, "Do you suppose either of us will ever cry again?"

"Not," she said, "unless it is something really important."

Cooper and Serena discussed setting up an online edition of the newspaper. She said she could have someone she knew at the school where she went to set it up for five hundred dollars. Cooper thought for a moment about it then told her he didn't want an online edition right now. Maybe after they had made the newspaper the best one he could, a paper everyone wanted to hold in their hand and read about what had happened in their county behind closed doors. Then he would think about it. They finished the weeks edition, re-read it through, discussed it, and Cooper said he was disappointed that he had nothing in it about the seven murders.

"You could have quoted the hot blonde," Serena said.

"Nothing she said was printable," he told her. He thought about it for a minute then said, "She talked about the caves on my mother's property and all through that area. What do you know about caves out there?"

"A lot of kids went into them. Not me, I hate caves.Snakes and bats . . .oooh!" She shivered. "Is that where she shot the video?"

He laughed. "Yeah, it was. Part of one anyway. You should have watched it. She was pole dancing on a stalactite. Or was it a stalagmite?"

"I'm sure it was entertaining," unable to conceal the sarcasm.

"I want to see the inside of the caves. She thought the caves were why Soldano wanted my mother's property and the others. I need someone to go in with me. How about later this week?"

"I don't do pole dancing," Serena said.

He laughed again. "No, no, not to shoot video. At least not of either one of us. Maybe the inside of the caves. See what's in there."

"No."

"That's an order. We go in the caves."

"I quit."

That surprised him. He looked at her and she stared back at him. "Please," he said. "I need you. Don't ever quit on me."

She looked at him long enough to make him nervous. "All right," she said. "I'll go in for five minutes. One time and never again."

"Okay. Day after tomorrow. Let's get the paper out, now."

When the printed copies were delivered back to them three hours later they sold sixty-one copies before closing and wrote fifteen new subscriptions. They both drank a beer before Serena rode off on her Triumph headed for night school. Cooper stood in the yard of the mobile home and watched her down the street and out of sight. Then he had another beer.

Bilbo—it had to be Bilbo according to Serena's description, scrawny, scruffy, half-beard, beady eyes, snake tattoos on his arm—looked up as Cooper entered the office of Bilbo's Exclusive Used Cars.

"Hey, Bro, what's up?" rising from his unnecessarily oversized office chair and thrusting his hand forward. Cooper took the hand—bony, smooth-skinned as if polished with a derma-stone—and smiled at him.

"Looking around," Cooper said. He saw a man approaching from the lot toward the office.

"You damn sure came to the right place," Bilbo said. "Whatcha got in mind? I got them all here on the lot. Your sporty ones, your executive ones, your all wheel drives. You name it partner, we'll go look at a few and drive anything you want."

"How about trade-ins? I got the old Toyota out there. Runs good."

"Yeah, yeah, I seen you drive up."

The man Cooper had seen walking toward the office came inside. He was stockily built, less than six feet in height, dressed casually but expensively—Polo emblem, upscale slacks. His hair was long and dark, tinged with gray, a massive wave sweeping from forehead back dominating his appearance. Something about him reminded Cooper of a 1950 gangster movie.

"Hey, Cody," Bilbo said, switching his attention from Cooper. "You know this guy, don't you? He's the new editor at the paper here."

Cooper, a bit surprised that Bilbo recognized him, looked at the man who stared back at him with an offhand casualness—much like the clothes he wore—and offered his hand. Cooper felt a strength when they gripped and he had the feeling of being contested by the man's strength. The man's eyes signaled a sense of superiority.

"Cody Wicker," the man said. "Didn't catch the name."

"Cooper Rease," Bilbo said quickly, "You know, the editor. Boss of the little Mexican girl comes around for ads."

"You the salesman?" Cooper asked Wicker, knowing who he

was and what he did around the used car lot. And in the county.

Wicker grinned, gave one final squeeze to Cooper's hand and seemed to toss it aside. "I keep Bilbo from giving the place away," he said, went over to Bilbo's refrigerator and extracted a can of the new beer-margarita mix. He held it out to Cooper and reached inside for another.

"What I really came here for," Cooper said, ignoring the offered can which Wicker set on the desk and opened his own can, "was to meet you guys. Ask some questions."

"This an interview for the newspaper?" Bilbo asked. He nervously reached for the can Wicker had set on the desk, looked at it, then put it back in the refrigerator. Cooper watched him, judging him, in no hurry.

"This is for my own satisfaction," he said. "I'm looking for the person or persons who blew up my office."

"Ah," Bilbo said, plastering his face with a false grin. "You're looking for Cody to help you, then. He's a private investigator."

"Let's start with you," Cooper said. He kept Bilbo under scrutiny but watching Wicker peripherally. "Fire marshal says it was dynamite. Background check says you ran into trouble in South Missouri. Some car shop was blown up with dynamite."

"Damn," Bilbo slammed a hand on his desk top. "That framed up charge keeps dogging me. Listen," he turned to Cooper holding a hand palm up, "I sure hope you don't put that in the paper. Man makes one mistake it hounds him for life. I like your little Mex girl, I'm planning on stepping up my ad campaign. I'm asking for a little slack here."

"This isn't about what goes in the newspaper. I'm naturally a little touchy about people blowing up my place of business. I could have been inside. I want to know who did it and why. So, I start with people who might know."

"Don't start with me," Bilbo pleaded. "I got no reason to blow your office up. Hell, I'm glad to see a new man in there. Paper needed somebody. Last one in here was a dud."

"What I mean to do here," Cooper said, "is to find out who killed the seven people. So, I figure whoever did it doesn't want me around. Grant Borden was the first one killed before the hog farm came here. His place was dynamited before he supposedly shot himself in the head twice."

"Hell, I didn't know that," Bilbo said. He turned to Wicker. "You know that about Borden, Cody?"

Wicker took a drink from his can nonchalantly. "Who's Grant Borden?"

"An old man set his house on fire then shot himself," Bilbo said. Turned back to Cooper. "Least that's what the authorities say."

Cooper turned to leave, opened the door, turned back, "Now you know what I'm going to do here. You hear anything, let me know."

Closing the door he saw Wicker raise his can in Cooper's direction and grin haughtily.

Carmello Stonebridge and Strefan Robensen came into the mobile home without knocking.

"This your office now?" she asked. Looking around, stopping for an instant with her eyes on Serena, then, "Quite a dump. And here I thought it wasn't possible to sink lower than a hundred-year-old gas station."

"Nice to see you again, Carmello," Cooper said. "You too, Strefan. You came by to cheer us up with praise and compliments?"

Carmello looked around for a chair to fit her, didn't find one so she pulled a stool that was close to Cooper and settled herself on it making it look insufficient for the occasion.

"You're getting no place fast," she said. "Who cares about a damn silo blowing up besides the farmer and a few cows. Strefan's got something to tell you."

Strefan, still in her nurses' uniform, stood clasping both hands in front of her, a slight smile on her face.

"Carmello has a way of getting right to the point," Strefan said. "I work at County Hospital, you know. Not really run by the county, of course. Non-profit company that piles up fourteen percent profit, but that's not what Carmello meant. County doesn't interfere with the operation nor does the federal government. Records are—how shall I put this—kept indiscriminately. In otherwords, there's no system to them."

"Sounds like a story there, maybe," Cooper said. "What have you found out?"

"Cecilia Roth—she was your mother, right? She had lung cancer."

Something twitched inside Cooper. "I didn't know. I didn't think she smoked. But, then, I didn't know much of anything about her, sad as that may sound."

"She didn't smoke," Carmello said. "Tell him the rest of it, Strefan. Elsie Loring had lung cancer, too. My mother. And I know damned well she didn't smoke."

"We've got a record of several cases of lung cancer from people who didn't smoke," Strefan said. "The only connection we've found that ties them all together is the caves on your mother's farm."

Before he could ask, Carmello said, "Just a guess, but Mom talked a lot about your mother and how she held regular events inside her cave. She served food there. And drinks. And it seems, from what I found out by asking relatives and the people themselves, a lot of the people diagnosed were regulars. They attended these events in your mother's cave. She derived a modest income from those events. We think there's something inside there causing it."

"What could that be?" Cooper asked.

Strefan said, "Radiation most likely. Maybe from radon poisoning. Second only to cigarettes as the cause for lung cancer."

Cooper was silent as he thought about what they had said. Carmello got off the stool, went to the refrigerator, opened it, brought out three beers stacked on top of each other, gave one to Strefan, set one in front of Cooper and opened the third and took a drink. She looked at Serena and said, "You're too young."

"How does all this tie in with Soldano and the hog farm and the other six people?" Cooper asked.

"You're the hotshot journalist," Carmello said. "You want a list of the people?" She turned to Strefan. "Give him the list, Sweetheart."

Strefan pulled a paper from a pocket on her uniform. "Had to write it out. Records at County aren't digitized."

Cooper took the paper, looked at it and passed it on to Serena. She looked it over and said, "I'm already feeling too sick to go with you into the caves tomorrow."

20

They didn't get in to the caves. No admission, Cooper was told. He tried calling Ev Miehle, but of course he wasn't available. Cooper decided to make the two hour drive to Soldano headquarters in St. Louis. Starting early he got to the plant at eight o'clock. He went through a half dozen people before he decided on a different tactic.

"I'm here to see Marla," he said. Surprisingly, the pretty, young receptionist said, "Just a moment," dialed a number and said into the phone, "A Mister Cooper Rease of a newspaper . . ." looking again at the paper he had written for her . . . "I think it's called," looking up at Cooper for affirmation, "the Special Edition."

Listening, then saying to Cooper, "One moment, they're checking for Marla."

Listening again, then, "All right, I'll send him right up."

To Cooper after putting the phone away, "Go to room 800. Elevators are to your right."

The reception room in 800 had more square footage than the entire Cluster County courthouse. A young man, thirtyish, handsome, Armani suit, silk tie, sat behind a long, sleek counter-desk with no ornamentation showing.

"Mister Rease?" he asked. He rose, went to one of several doors behind him that probably cost more than Cooper paid for his newspaper, and with his hand on what could have been a solid gold doorknob, said, "Right this way, Miss Gilbert's expecting you."

Cooper entered a suite more elaborate than his imagination could have conjured up. Everything in sight would have cost more than any house in Cluster County. Marla sat on a sofa that was plush, and extended for probably twenty feet. She smiled at him, did not rise, but patted the puffed, leather encased cushion beside her.

"Mister Rease, how nice to see you again. Please have a seat. Ev's off to Italy on business—and some pleasure, you can bet," followed by a laugh.

He sat carefully, the cushion feeling as if it had no bottom. She was so different from the person he had remembered at the hog facility. There she had been tentative, preening to Ev Miehle, almost frightened.

Cooper thanked her for seeing him, explaining he had driven down for the visit and hoped it had not interfered with her busy schedule.

"Not at all. How about coffee, tea or what pleases you. Perhaps some Danish to go along with it. You're probably famished after such a long drive."

He agreed and Marla pulled a smart phone from her pocket, swiped her finger on the face of it, tapped and said, "Della, some refreshments, please."

She put the phone away and looked back at Cooper with sparkling eyes. That was what was so different about her, he decided.The eyes. No black-rimmed, plastic glasses. At the hog farm she appeared as a farmer's wife. Here, in all this elegance, she looked like a person who belonged in such surroundings.

The Special Edition

"Nice place you have here," he told her. "I could put my whole newspaper operation in your office, press and all, and have room left over for a two bedroom condo."

She laughed, a bit phony, he thought. "Soldano treats me rather well. And I appreciate it."

"I apologize, but I didn't catch your function. I guess Ev didn't give it much thought."

"Typical," she said, still smiling.

He waited, but she added nothing. "And what you actually do for Soldano is . . . what?"

"Public relations," she said quickly and dismissed it with a wave of her hand. "Oh, here comes Della." A young black woman followed a silver and walnut cart into the room loaded with coffee pots, elegant china, piles of rolls and donuts, napkins and sparkling silverware pieces. Marla directed her where to place the cart and Della began pouring coffee in cups trimmed with a gold rim. She placed a filled cup on an elaborate saucer with a silver spoon and handed it with a cloth, linen napkin to Cooper. While she completed the serving, Cooper nibbled a Danish, drank the strong, black coffee and waited to see where Marla would take the situation.

While sipping her coffee daintily, she told Della to contact a name to arrange a tour of the plant for Mister Rease. Cooper didn't object. He was curious about the operation.

After more refreshments and exchanged pleasantries, Marla excused herself from the plant tour just as another upscale young man entered and was introduced by Marla as James. Before leaving with James, Cooper told Marla about being denied access to the hog farm, explaining he wanted to see his mother's house. She didn't understand. Who was his mother? Where was her house? Why hadn't he told Ev about his mother? Where was she now?

After he had answered all of her questions truthfully, Marla became a different person. She appeared very nervous, even wringing her hands. Much like the woman he had met at the hog farm, except she was now in appearance quite different. No plain hair style, no dowdy dress. As he walked away with James she stood almost in shock.

As he wondered about her and about the change that had come over her, he followed James and got a complete tour of the plant. The tour turned out to be quite interesting. Soldano's main function was chemical rendering of grain seeds to resist the chemical herbicide Soldano processed that farmers applied to their fields before planting. Cooper asked James about the hog farm and how that fit in with what they did at the plant here.

"I'll have to refer you to someone else," James said. "All I know is we do some testing with the grain before the agricultural department and the FDA grants permission to market the seed. I believe we did some testing using pigs. Pigs are apparently very close to humans in the regards of digestion and so forth. Please, no jokes, but that's my understanding. So maybe a decision was made to raise our own pigs or maybe we had a lot of pigs left over and nothing to do with them. I really can't answer that. I know Mister Miehle—Ev, not Ernest—likes pigs. Can't get enough of them. Has a big cutout of Porky Pig on his office wall."

"What's the name of the project where you tested grain with the pigs?" Cooper asked.

James thought a moment. "Stolid, I think it was. No, wait, that's not it. Standard, that's it. Or, I think it is. Sorry, I'll have to brush up on that end of it. I can get you some literature that explains it better than I can and it will be correct. Unlike me."

The tour took an hour and James returned him to the original reception room where he had started. The pretty young receptionist asked him to wait after he had shaken James' hand and was preparing to ask about Marla again.

"Mister Miehle wants to speak with you," she said.

"From Italy?" he asked, but without answering she said into a sleek, black telephone receiver, "Here's Mister Rease," and handed it to him.

He said hello and heard Ev Miehle's voice. "Cooper? Damn glad you could visit us. Sorry I'm not there, we could share some drinks. It's happy hour over here. Damn Italians and their dago red. Good food, though. My god, I've never eaten better. Marla contacted me, she was concerned about you wanting to see your mother's house. Really touched her. Tell me about it. Hell, I didn't know you had a personal connection to the farm."

"Cecilia Roth," Cooper said. "She was murdered in her home there. I wanted to see if her house was still standing. Walk around her place."

"Hell yes, you can. I'm not familiar with the place you're talking about, and sadly, I don't know anything about her or what happened there. Damn shame if that's what it was. I'll look into it. Listen, I'll get somebody to escort you to where she lived. They'll be contacting you."

"Let me give you my number," Cooper said.

"I'll find you. Glad you could visit the plant. You need anything else, get hold of Marla. *Chow* as they say over here or is it *river dare che*."

Ev Miehle was gone. Cooper had not considered himself

important enough for one of the richest men in the country to interrupt a visit to Italy to call him. What was it about his mother's property?

And the caves?

21

Serena had left a stack of stuff she had printed online on the kitchen counter he used for his desk. He looked them over and saw they were from the *Kansas City Star*. They had published their own special edition on agricultural subsidies paid out in the whole state. She limited the copies to payouts in Cluster County. Fifteen. Number one was Soldano Agriculture Enterprise, $240,000. Number two was Grady Quichen, $110,000. The same Grady Quichen who was the Farm Services Agency director for Cluster County and the man who had approved the Soldano hog farm.

Carmello answered his call immediately with a, "You got Carmello. What's up?"

"Cooper Rease, *Special Edition*. I just got a printout from the *Kansas City Star* about the agricultural subsidies in the county. The hog farm got the most then our friend Quichen with $110,000. What do you know about that?"

"Well, well, well," she said. "Interesting. I've got a stack of gobble-de-gook from my FOI request. Quichen approved the hog farm request and the loan without an approval from the EPA. Our corrupt state environmental okayed it, supposed to have sent it on to the EPA for final approval only EPA has no record of it."

"Have you talked with the state people?"

"Yeah. Inadequate staff to do an investigation. Hired a consultant who was—they say—federally certified."

"Got a name?"

"Martin Dinsmore."

Cooper could almost feel the thought colliding with memory inside his head. "Did I hear you right? Martin Dinsmore?"

"The same. Remember him? Died unspecified causes inside his car parked in the town of New Port."

Cooper said, "I believe they suspected rat poison. So now we know how the hog farm got approved. But, can we prove anything?"

"Up to you, journalistic hotshot. I gotta run, my bell's ringing off the wall. Still in my candy stripes. Hope to read all about it in the *Special Edition*."

"This is a message for Mister Cooper Rease. You have requested a guided tour of zone 87 of the Soldano Agricultural Farm in Cluster County. Someone will meet you at the main entrance to the farm at one-thirty p.m. tomorrow for the tour that will last one hour. The next available guided tour date would be thirty days from now. If you are able to make the date tomorrow press one. If you are unable to make the date, press two. Goodbye."*

"A damn robo call," Cooper muttered. He checked the time, nine-thirty. Dark outside. Serena should be out of her evening class by now so he called her phone. It went to voice mail.

"Got your wish, Soldano gave me a robo call. One thirty tomorrow afternoon for a tour of the hog farm and beautiful caves. Wear something suitable."

Suitable turned out to be a pair of bib overalls—probably her fathers—over a black turtleneck jersey under a hooded jacket.

He looked her over deliberately and said, "There goes the office dress code." She stuck her tongue out at him.

At the front gate to the Soldano Agricultural Farm, Cooper told his name to the speaker by the gate, waited, then heard, "Proceed along the main route to the farrowing houses following the signs to Road K, turn on Road W and proceed to the house with a sign in front saying Zone 16. You will be met there by your guide. Do not proceed on any other route."

"Friendly," Serena observed. The gate opened and Cooper followed instructions given by the voice over the speaker. Serena said, "P-U," and pulled the turtle neck jersey over her nose.

Cooper gave her a running ramble about pigs and farms and bacon, anything to get a laugh from her, but he failed. He got to the small house, yellow with white shudders and doorway and the sign in front with Zone 16 on it. The man standing by a black Mercedes was the tall, muscular man he had seen at the barns when he met Ev Miehle. Cooper got out of the car, as did Serena, and walked to meet the man who stood with arms folded, signifying there would be no handshaking.

"You would be Jurgen Miehle," Cooper said to him.

"That's right," Jurgen nodded and looked Serena over. She had lowered the jersey now and her face and hair were uncovered.

"You're our guide?" Cooper asked.

"I didn't know there would be two of you," Jurgen said, still looking at Serena.

"Serena, my assistant," Cooper told him. "Shall we go on in the house?"

"I was told it was your mother's. I can allow you to look

around. No entrance, of course." Jurgen hadn't moved since they drove up.

"Not what your father told me," Cooper said. He walked toward the house and Jurgen fell in behind him. "What's so secret about her house? She was killed inside, you know. I want to see where it happened."

Jurgen walked past him up to the door into the house. He tried the latch and the door opened. "Wait here," he said and went inside closing the door behind him.

Serena, now beside Cooper, said, "You sure you want to see this?"

"I'm sure," he said, opened the door and went in.

The house was modest, three rooms and a bath from what was visible from the door. Cooper was two steps inside when Jurgen came into the small living room from one of the two doorways on the opposite wall.

"You don't take directions well, do you?" he said.

Cooper didn't answer. He looked around at a small sofa, two armchairs, a small claw-foot dining table with two chairs. The room smelled musty and dust particles hung in the air, stirred up by steps on the carpeting. He walked around the room, looking at the pictures on the walls of farm scenes and Norman Rockwell magazine covers in worn frames. He sat on the sofa, heard the springs buckling, and tried to remember his mother. Jurgen walked past and from the doorway said, "We have to leave in fifteen minutes."

Cooper rose from the sofa, looked at Serena who was watching him, and said, "I wish I had known her. I wish I hadn't been such a damn fool."

He walked through one of the doors into a bedroom and saw

the bed and saw the blood on the floor and one smear on the wall. The bed had a colorful quilt crumpled on it and two pillows askew. A six drawer dresser stood against one wall. Two framed pictures sat on the top, one was of Clay, probably the day he graduated from college. The other was of the family before the divorce. Cooper was about six, his father stood next to his mother, both smiling into the camera, and Clay on the side opposite Cooper. He held it in his hand for some minutes, then set it back. He began going through the drawers, surprised that anything was left in them, or in the house for that matter. Had Clay not come to his mother's house after her death? Took nothing in remembrance? Had his mother died with no one loving her or even caring?

In one drawer, a stack of papers caught his attention and he began going through them. Some of them were bank records Cooper thought Clay would have wanted, others were of bills and tax records on the property and one manilla envelop marked personal. He opened it and found a letter written in a hand he recognized. His own. A letter he had written his mother a year after he had told her he hated her. Just now he remembered writing it, but decided not to mail it. He read through his own juvenile thoughts where he apologized for being hateful and telling her he still loved her and wished he still lived with her. It was signed, "Your loving son, Cooper Rease."

He sensed Serena standing beside him. He handed her the letter. She read it, then placed a hand on his arm. "See," she said, "you didn't need to cry after all. You did the right thing, you sent her the letter."

"I wrote it, but I didn't mail it. My father must have mailed it." He folded it and stuck it in his pocket. "I've seen enough, our time is up."

Jurgen waited, propped against the Mercedes. "Go back the same way," he said. "I'll follow you."

"I wanted to see the caves," Cooper said. "She held a lot of parties in the caves."

"What caves?" Jurgen asked.

The ones you and Lisa Allen cavorted naked in and videoed your sex exploits in, Cooper thought, but said instead, "The caves that were part of her ten acres. I'm sure you know about them."

"I wasn't told anything about any caves," Jurgen told him without moving from his position against the automobile or unfolding his arms.

"Well, I'm saying it now," Cooper told him, coming up to stand in front of the hard-jawed Jurgen. "If you want, we can call your father."

"Won't be necessary. The caves, if there are any, are off limits to the public."

"And why is that?"

"Today the why is because I said so."

Cooper took out his phone and called the number he had recorded for Soldano's office in St. Louis. He asked the first receptionist for Ev Miehle and gave his name. After holding for a minute was told Mr. Miehle wasn't available. He asked for Marla Gilbert, another wait, and again was told she wasn't available either. He put the phone away and looked at Jurgen.

"Shall we go?" Jurgen said and got in the Mercedes.

222

They received the courthouse reports again, this time in the mailbox on the street in front of the mobile home. Although Cooper had nailed up a crude sign in the yard in front, Serena was surprised the courthouse mole knew where to leave the reports. She went through them, made some notes, called a couple of people in the reports and verified their authenticity. Two of the sheets were different. She looked them over and brought them to Cooper who sat at his kitchen-counter desk.

"Interesting," she told him, laying them in front of him.

He looked at the papers, one a copy of an order to Arrowhead Trucking for delivery to a restaurant chain in Omaha, Nebraska for three hundred pounds of bacon and ham. The other was a copy of a bill from Soldano Agricultural Farm for the meat with a note written with marker pen on the bill, "MEAT IS UNSUITABLE."

"Let's see if we can talk with this restaurant chain in Omaha," Cooper said.

Serena returned to her own work space and placed the call. Within minutes she told Cooper that the purchasing agent for the chain was on the phone.

Cooper identified himself and made reference to the bill from Soldano on the rejected meat.

"I recall that," the agent said. "Something strange about the meat. Was too fatty for one thing. Different color and texture. We started dispensing it anyway, but we got inspected and the meat was rejected."

"Who inspected you?" Cooper asked.

"Wait, I've got the report in file here." He was silent for a moment before returning to the phone. "Yeah, here it is. John Markham. Food and Drug Administration. He sent samples to some laboratory. Here's another paper, this one from the laboratory. Says the sample is radioactive beyond the threshold. So we sent it back. Never heard another word from them."

"Did you tell them what was wrong with the meat?"

"Don't recall they asked. We just told them it was not suitable for our needs. I can check with some of the other people here, but I don't recall any response from Soldano."

"Could you send me copies of the laboratory report?" Cooper asked.

"I'll have to check with management. Wouldn't want you printing in your newspaper that our chain serves radioactive bacon on our BLT's."

"I won't give your name, I protect my sources," Cooper said.

"I'll check," the man said. "If I send you a copy we'll have to redact our name and the name of the FDA and the lab."

"I would like to receive whatever you feel comfortable with. I will probably write about this, but you can be assured I won't be mentioning any names except Soldano."

"Don't expect too much," the man said and ended the call.

Cooper told Serena what he had found out. "You heard Carmello say my mother and her mother had cancer. Could it have come from exposure from some radioactive source at the hog farm, I wonder."

"How does that tie in with the caves?" Serena said. "Now I'm itching all over. I had to take three showers to get rid of the smell, now how do I get rid of the radioactivity?"

"I've got to get inside those caves," he said.

"I can't do that," Serena said and shuddered. "I can't go with you."

"Then you're fired," he said, reached over and patted her on the head. "And hired again. Just wanted to remind you who's the boss around here."

"I know who's the boss," she said, and by her tone it was evident she didn't mean Cooper. "Now get to work writing this up for this week's paper."

"Yes boss," he said.

The phone rang, Serena answered, listened, looked at Cooper and said, "For you, boss."

"Cooper Rease," he said into the phone.

"I checked with the management," the purchasing agent he had talked with said. "I was mistaken, there are no records of rejected meat orders from anyone. We don't have any laboratory reports on file, just in case you get involved in any libel suits. I misspoke, I was mistaken. There are no records."

"Hmm," Cooper mused. "Cold feet, huh? You're not a very good citizen. What if I advise my readers not to eat in your restaurants or they might become radioactive?"

"We get lots of crackpot complaints," the man said. "Soldano is a good customer of ours. I'm sure they would join us in any lawsuit that might occur."

The call ended.

"That didn't take long," he told Serena. "Soldano has a long reach. We've been threatened. Again."

Carmello helped him locate Harry Atkins, a local spelunker, though he had no idea how she did it. He called the number she gave him, a land-line phone with an answering machine. He left his number. Within minutes the man returned his call, identifying himself very business-like. Cooper asked if he was a caver and got an affirmative.

"My mother owned ten acres on what is now the Soldano Agricultural Farm," Cooper told Atkins. "I'm looking for someone who may have been in the caves on her property and who might want to go back inside them."

"I've explored about every cave in that area," Atkins said. "What was your mother's name?"

Cooper told him and the man said, "Oh, yeah, she was the woman had tea parties inside the big cave on her place. I've been in there. Even had tea with her one day."

"Would you be willing to go back inside?" Cooper asked.

"Way I understand, those caves are off limits to the public. I talked with them at that stinking hog farm and they chased me off. Even gave me a mild threat, like we'll throw you in jail if you try it."

"Yeah, they pretty much said the same to me. Look, I'll be up front with you. The hospital says my mother had lung cancer. I hadn't seen her in years, sadly, so I don't know to what extent her condition was. I wanted to know if there was something in the cave that caused her cancer. Something radioactive."

"Hmm," Atkins said. "So you think maybe the caves have

something radioactive in them? Like uranium?"

"Yeah, something like that. Have you ever run into something in any of the caves?"

"Oh, sure. Uranium is one of the more plentiful elements. Found in small quantities everywhere. I usually take a meter with me, a Geiger counter. I almost always get a signal. I'm a chemist so I'm always curious about what can be found under the ground. You'd be surprised."

"What's your opinion of my theory?"

"Not likely. I probably had my meter with me when I was in there with your mother, but I don't specifically recall that."

"So, there's no way I could check it out for sure."

Atkins was thinking. "Have you ever done any caving?"

"Not something I ever had a desire to do."

"The only way you could get inside those caves on her property is by going in the ones off the farm. About a mile away straight across, but about two miles underground. That whole area is linked up with tunnels, underground rivers, springs, the whole works. Someone like me, with experience might be able to do it, walking, crawling, maybe even swimming, but for a non-caver like you, no way."

"Unless I had a guide. An experienced spelunker like you."

Atkins laughed. "I'm not for hire, sorry. Knees are bad, back gives me problems. Sorry."

"Anyone you could suggest?"

Atkins thought about it and said, "No, no one in my group. We're all about the same age. You'd need a young one for that job."

"I think there's a tie in with Soldano and the hog farm," Cooper said. "I think the whole operation is a threat to the community and even beyond. I'm a crusader, I'll admit. Most news men are. Wish I could find a combination, part news man and part spelunker."

Atkins laughed again. "Well, if that's all you're looking for, try old Dan Hargrove. He's written books on about every cave in the world. Trouble is, he's older even than I am."

"You know him well?"

"Sure, we've crawled on our bellies together in a lot of places."

Cooper said, "Don't suppose you would appeal to him for me?"

"You're really serious about this, aren't you."

"Yes, I am."

Atkins cleared his throat, waited, then said, "Well, what the hell is a couple of sore knees. I'll check with Dan. If he's game, so am I. I'll get back to you, leave me your number."

"I'd like to go with you," Cooper said.

"Whoa, bad enough without an amateur along."

"If I fall behind you have my permission to just leave me."

Cooper waited.

"We'll see," Atkins said. "Leave me your number."

After he laid his phone down, Serena looked at him.

"I'm in," he said. "I'm going inside that damn cave."

223

Cooper was dressed for it. Harry Atkins had read off a list of equipment and clothing: boots, tight-fitting dungarees, goggles, gloves. He met two men on the highway Atkins had mentioned. The first man out of the Ford pickup was tall and bookish looking. His all-white hair signaled his age, but other than that he didn't look as old as he had led Cooper to believe.

The second man dismounting was short with white hair also along with an inch long beard and mustache nearly as long. That, Cooper believed, would be the caver-writer, Dan Hargrove.

Cooper introduced himself to the first man who was, indeed, Harry Atkins. Atkins looked Cooper over with a grin, commented on his outfit and handed him a hard hat with a light on the front. He showed Cooper how to use it, then turned to introduce Hargrove who seemed all business. He gave Cooper a short handshake, looked him over, then said to Atkins, "Be easier if he stays behind."

"He's insistent," Atkins told him. "He gave us permission to leave him behind if he's a laggard.

"Hmmph," Hargrove said. He produced a roll of slick-looking paper and started to unroll the sheets. "Waterproof," he said. Cooper knew that was for his benefit to know. "Now," Hargrove went on, "I've mapped some of this and some others have mapped some of it. So, most of it is mapped. The only challenge is to follow the maps."

He looked at Cooper, "I'll keep the maps. I'll lead, you will follow me and Harry will bring up the rear. You'll be able to see me and my Maglite. Just keep up. I'll try and announce all the passageways as we come to them and all the difficult crossings. Keep your gloves on, don't touch the things I tell you not to touch. There's a good reason for it."

Cooper nodded. "I'll try not to be a burden."

"Let's get started, then," Hargrove said. He marched straight for the depression in the ground and came to a wrought iron gate about four feet tall. Hargrove used a key to unlock the padlock and entered the opening on his knees. He handed the key to Cooper and said "Pass it back to Harry so he can lock up after us. Don't want a bunch of strangers coming in behind us."

They crawled about twenty feet and came to a large open area where they could stand up. Their lights sparkled off the limestone formations in the opening. The temperature inside was mild, about sixty degrees, Cooper guessed. Pleasant.

Cooper saw Hargrove point to some formations as they walked past. "Don't touch," he said. "Cave bacon."

Cooper couldn't help marveling at the limestone formations. In places his light picked up water dripping off formations. Hargrove was moving faster than Cooper thought they would have been able to. Cooper was too rushed to take in sights he had never seen before or could even imagine. Harry Atkins, probably knowing how he felt, said behind him, "Almost a miracle, eh. Such beauty. People ask why I'm a caver. If they could see this they wouldn't ask."

Hargrove came to an almost a blank wall. A space existed between two vertical walls seemingly only a foot apart. Hargrove said, "If you can feel the air flow, that's a passage."

They did manage to squeeze through the passageway and Hargrove announced, "Water," and Cooper was in up to nearly the top of his boots. They came out into another passage that resembled a creek with broken ice along its walls. Next they walked in some mud the consistency of peanut butter spiked with water. Hargrove held up a hand, held a sheet of his map in front of his helmet light, then said, "Okay, here's where we have to do the knuckle crawl for about thirty yards."

They came into another passageway that led to a waterfall cascading over smooth rocks as large as automobiles.

"We get a tick every so often on the Geiger," Atkins said at one juncture. "Nothing out of the ordinary."

Close to an hour had expired when they came to a large rock formation with a flat area on top.

"Let's take a break," Hargrove announced and settled himself on the rock. Cooper was exhausted. He was surprised at the endurance of both the older men. He began thinking how he needed to get himself in better shape.

Hargrove had his waterproof map sheets spread out on the flat rock and was inspecting them.

"How close are we?" Cooper asked.

Hargrove ran a finger along one of the maps and said, "About ten, maybe fifteen minutes. Pretty smooth going now except for one tight spot. You'll learn to belly crawl."

"I can't get over the colors," Cooper said. "Such brilliant oranges and even blacks. Must be every mineral in the world inside here.'

"Quite a few," Atkins told him. "Caves are full of organisms you can't find anywhere else on earth. The grotto sculpin is one.

Lots of endangered species inside the caves, too."

Hargrove unwrapped a chocolate bar and started munching. "Diabetes," he told Cooper. "You don't want me passing out in here."

About ten minutes after they had resumed their exploration, Hargrove pulled up short. "What's that smell?" Then answered himself, "That's manure. Pure shit. Can't be the bats, they don't smell like that." He looked back at Atkins. "What do you make of it, Harry?"

Atkins said, "It smells like hog manure. Pig shit. And my counter is going crazy. I've been in this part before. I never had more than a tick on my Geiger."

"What the hell have they done, pumped their hog waste in the caves?" Hargrove said.

"How close are we to where we're going?" Cooper asked.

"Close," Atkins said. "I know this section. Something has changed since I was in here."

"By God, if they're dumping waste in the caves, that stuff will run all the way to the Mississippi. That's got to be stopped."

"If it's just pig shit, why is it radioactive?" Atkins said.

Hargrove turned and his helmet light was in Cooper's face. "Let's get the hell out of here," he said and squeezed past Cooper to take the lead back over the passageway they had just come through.

Cooper heard Atkins' Geiger counter then clicking like a cricket. His own helmet light shined on Atkins' face and he saw a bit of fear there.

"I'm glad I missed the trip into the caves," Serena said to Cooper as he sat at the counter staring into space. "Especially the piggy poop part. Got enough of that the other day at your mother's house."

"I actually enjoyed it up to then." Cooper opened his third beer since returning from the cave expedition. "You should see the colors inside the caves. Like nothing you've ever seen before. The limestone formations are something man will never be able to duplicate."

"I'll take your word for it. Take any pictures?"

"Yeah, I did. They're in the camera, take a look. But the pictures don't do justice."

"So what are your cave explorers going to do about the hog waste inside the pristine caves?"

"Hargrove, that's the old guy, he was really pissed. He's going to get the Speleogical—or something like that—people to take it to the environmental people or the governor or somebody. Then Atkins, that's the guy Carmello dug up for me, he says how are we going to complain about it when we're trespassing. So Hargrove says to hell with that. We're not going to let a bunch of hog crap destroy half the caves in the state and half the water streams and springs."

He took a long swig from his beer, set it down and said, "I

don't know what they can do to tell you the truth. Somehow I've got to find out where the radioactivity is coming from, if that's what gave my mother cancer and is Soldano causing it."

"Didn't the meat that was rejected by the restaurant chain in Omaha test positive for radioactivity?" Serena ask.

"Yeah, you're right. But how can we tie the two together. Where do you suppose our mole got the rejection paper from the restaurant?"

"It must have been in the files somewhere in the courthouse. But why?"

Cooper said, "If the meat was radioactive, then so were the hogs. It must have come from what the hogs ate. Genetically modified grain from Soldano. If the hogs were radioactive, then their waste would be radioactive. So if they dump the waste in the caves or in a stream that runs into the caves, then that's what Atkins was picking up on his Geiger counter. He's a chemist so he starts talking about half-life, thorium, uranium, radon. He says it depends on the decay time, whatever that means. I barely passed chemistry. How about you?"

"What's chemistry?" she deadpanned.

"My sentiments exactly. But I'm going to have to read up on it. Let's try and trace the lab report through the FDA. See if you can find the office that this guy John Markham worked at. I'll give them a call."

The search took Serena four minutes. When Cooper threw his empty in the trash and went to the refrigerator, she said, "I made coffee."

He stood thinking about it, his hand on the refrigerator door, then got a cup and poured it full of coffee.

His call was routed several times before he was connected

with the meat inspection division. He asked the woman for John Markham and was told no one worked in that division by that name.

"I need to talk with someone about a laboratory test Mister Markham conducted two years ago," Cooper said.

"You're with the news media?" the woman asked.

"Yes, the newspaper *Special Edition* in New Port."

"You can obtain that information through the Freedom of Information Act," she told him. "I wouldn't be able to access that information without authority to do so."

"Why is that?" Cooper asked without keeping the edge from his voice.

"Confidential proprietary information," she said. "Part of the rules."

"Maybe I could talk with the supervisor," Cooper said.

"Of course. I'll transfer you to Mister Ellsworth's desk."

"Was Mister Ellsworth the supervisor two years ago?"

"No that would have been Miss Gilbert. She's no longer with this division."

Ding, ding. Bells went off inside Cooper's head. "Would that have been Miss Marla Gilbert?"

"Yes, that's correct. Just a moment for the transfer. You'll be on hold."

The line went silent. Cooper waited. An excitement grew inside. So, Marla Gilbert the supervisor in the FDA when they lab tested Soldano Farm's hog meat and found it radioactive, now worked for Soldano. Doing nothing in an elaborate office with perks galore. Interesting.

A woman came on the phone and when Cooper asked for Mister Ellsworth he was told he was not available and asked if he wished to leave a message or a request to be called.

"Well, I was actually looking for Miss Marla Gilbert, but I understand Mister Ellsworth took her place. Where did she go? A transfer?"

"I think she retired to go into private business," the woman said.

"Maybe I could talk with John Markham, then if Mister Ellsworth is not available."

"Mister Markham no longer works here. He died about eighteen months ago."

"Oh, no. Sorry to hear that. What was the cause of death. I hadn't heard."

"I believe it was cancer," she said.

"All right, thanks for your help. I don't care to leave a message."

Laying the phone down, he said to Serena, "John Markham died of cancer and the woman he worked for, Marla Gilbert, now works for Soldano."

"The plot thickens," she said.

The call woke him at two a.m. Serena asked, "Are you awake?"

He mumbled, "Yes."

"Get over to my parents' house right away," and terminated the call.

He couldn't find his shoes, his pants were left in a chair or on the floor, dammit. He stumbled out the door hoping he had found all of his clothes and most of all, the keys to the Toyota.

Starting out after cranking the engine long enough to run down the battery almost, he tried to remember the streets to the Gonzalez house in his half-awake state. When he got there—reasonably sure it was the right place—Serena came out the front door and waved him inside. There he found both her parents in their nightclothes and a young man who looked to be of Mexican extraction lying on the sofa bleeding.

Serena was pushing Cooper toward the young man with cuts on his face and a loose piece of skin drooping over one eye. Clearly he had been beaten badly.

"Jimmy Rodriquez," Serena said. "Clustermole. He's the night janitor at the courthouse. He got caught tonight at the courthouse. They beat him up."

Cooper got a closer look at the young man in his early twenties. "He needs a doctor," Cooper said. "Call the ambulance."

"It's better if we take him," Serena said. "Some of the EMTs are friends of Bilbo and Wicker."

"You think they did this?"

"I know they did." She leaned down to talk with the injured young man. "Jimmy, tell Cooper what happened, then we've got to get you to the hospital."

Rosalind Gonzalez placed a damp cloth over the Jimmy Rodriquez' damaged eye and handed him a glass of water, then placed two pills in his hand. He struggled to sit partly upright, held the cloth in placed and took the pills.

He looked at Cooper. "They'd installed surveillance cameras, but I'd been getting around them, I knew how, but tonight Bilbo and Wicker had the assessor's office staked out. They caught me copying the files and worked me over."

"Jimmy is Jose Rodriquez' brother," Serena said, "the Arrowhead driver who was shot inside his cab. Jose gave him the papers about the rejected meat. He was the truck driver for that load."

"They killed him," Jimmy said. "I know they did. Bastards even bragged about it as they were beating me up."

"How did you get away?" Cooper asked.

"Tripped Bilbo into Wicker and ran. I hid in a storage closet they didn't know about. They cussed and yelled and stomped around for awhile, then I guess they thought I had gotten away outside so they left. I came here, didn't know where else to go. Not to the sheriff's that's for sure. I need to go before all of you get into trouble."

"Don't worry about that," Fernando Gonzalez said. "We need to get you patched up. Did they break any bones?"

"I don't think so. Wicker got me a couple of shots in the ribs. Bastard's mean as hell." He looked at Rosalind. "Excuse my language inside your house, Ma'm."

Rosalind waved off his apology. "We'd better get you to the hospital, now. You drove your car here, right?"

"Yeah. I can get to the hospital by myself, no need to get you involved. I just wanted Serena to know about it. That I won't be able to get the reports anymore."

"I'll drive him," Cooper said. "The rest of you better stay here. I'll see that he's taken care of. Will he be all right at the hospital?"

Serena said, "I think so. Maybe I better come with you. Jimmy and I go to the same evening class. He wants to be in law enforcement."

"We need some good people there, that's for sure," Cooper said. "I want you to stay here. Just in case we run into those two again."

"They'll be at the all night bar outside Cluster," Jimmy said. "I see Bilbo's fancy car there every night when I get off work. They hold some big-money card games there at night. He's one of the big-dollar players."

Cooper helped Jimmy into his Toyota, Rosalind Gonzalez giving him two more wet towels to hold on his injured eye. As Cooper closed his car door and started the engine, Serena signaled to roll down his window. She said "Be careful, boss. Be very careful."

Cooper left Jimmy in the care of two young nurses he seemed to know and an older doctor who told him he would need some stitches. As they were sewing and patching Jimmy, the doctor probed his rib cage and based on Jimmy's flinches from the doctor's fingers, he was told they would have to keep him overnight for x-rays the next day.

Cooper told the doctor that the people who assaulted Jimmy might come looking for him at the hospital. That he needed to be in a secure room and no one was to be told he was here.

"This needs to be reported to the authorities, then," the doctor said.

"That's where I'm going right now," Cooper said.

He found a deputy on duty at the sheriff's office. Cooper told him there had been an assault and that a young man had been beaten. He refused to give the deputy Jimmy's name and demanded the sheriff be called. The deputy was reluctant, but after some blustering and threatening, he called Sheriff Johnny Klemm.

Cooper waited in silence a half hour before the sheriff showed up. He told the sheriff he would like to talk with him in his office. The deputy looked amused and offended as Cooper walked past him following the sheriff into the his office.

Cooper started before the sheriff was fully behind his desk. He was a younger man than Walker Burnett, medium height, stocky, slightly red faced with short blond hair.

"A young man has been brutally beaten by Edward Bilbo and Cody Wicker. He was making copies of public records in the courthouse when the two men beat him up. I want the men arrested. If you don't, there's going to be one hell of an article in my newspaper this week."

Klemm started firing questions at Cooper about who the young man was and what right he had to be in the courthouse copying records. That sounded like something unlawful to him, but he would check into it. He didn't see the need to get rousted out of bed. Where was the young man now so that he could talk with him.

Cooper said, "A young man's life is in danger. He could easily have been killed. Would have been killed except he managed to escape from them. Bilbo and Wicker are at the Broken Bow bar outside town.Get out there and arrest them before they hunt this young man down and finish the job of killing him."

"I know how to handle my job . . ."

"Like hell you do," Cooper said. "You're falling into the same crooked rut Burnett was caught in. Don't start taking payoffs from Jack Stadler. Don't start down the wrong road. Do the right thing. Be somebody. Be a public servant, be on the people's side. Stand up and be somebody."

Cooper left, looking back at Klemm, at the perplexed look on his face, then headed back to his Toyota, started it and drove down the street that led to the Broken Bow.

26

Bilbo was shuffling cards when Cooper walked up to the darkened, run-down barroom with ten tables scattered around at random. One solitary light hung over the table where five men sat with bottles and glasses in front of them. Cody Wicker sat beside Bilbo A popcorn machine sat close to the table and some of the men had bowls beside their glasses and chips.

The door with two glass partitions at the top was locked when Cooper tried it. He raised his foot and kicked it open, the glass partitions shattering and falling on the floor. The five men at the table looked up and Bilbo rose quickly to his feet, the cards still in his hands.

"What the hell . . ." he said. Wicker turned in his chair and pushed his jacket aside, reaching a hand inside.

Cooper was at the popcorn machine in two strides. He reached inside the glass panels on the front of the machine, grabbed the wooden handle used to dump the kettle when done popping and pulled the whole kettle loose from it's magnetic latch and electrical plug. He advanced on the table of men and swung the kettle viciously toward Bilbo and Wicker who was in the act of rising from his chair. Hot grease slung out of the kettle, splattered on Wicker first, making a stripe across his jacket and on to Bilbo who wore only a thin, tropical flowered shirt over khakis. Wicker yelled as the hot grease hit him and Bilbo screamed with cards flying in the air. The table was kicked over in the rush of the others trying to escape the path of hot, flying grease.

As Cooper swung the hot kettle in a hack-handed stroke, Bilbo screamed again when more grease and hot popcorn kernels began splattering against his colorful shirt and his body. Wicker had come up with a pistol in his hand he had taken from inside his jacket, but when the hot kettle slammed into his hand the pistol went flying across the room. The other three men had run away from the path of the grease and were heading for the door.

Wicker yelled loudly as the kettle smacked against his hand, stumbled backwards into Bilbo who had fallen into his chair. Cooper swung the kettle again, popped popcorn flying in the air along with hot kernels and boiling oil. The kettle glanced off Wicker's shoulder before landing on his jaw or it would have smashed his face. He groaned loudly and slid to the floor.

Cooper gathered his hands and arms for another backhand swing of the kettle when Bilbo went over backwards crashing the chair he sat in. He crawled rapidly away from the table and headed for the door. As he got there, Sheriff Johnny Klemm came through. He caught Bilbo by the arm and Bilbo began crying and screaming that the son of a bitch was trying to kill him. The sheriff led Bilbo over to the fallen table with chips, glasses, bottles, bowls and cigarettes scattered around it. Wicker was yelling, pulling at his jacket soaked with hot oil and looking around for his pistol.

"Shut up," Sheriff Johnny Klemm yelled at him. "You two have done enough damage for one night. You're under arrest for assault, damage of property and a whole lot of other charges."

Wicker pulled off his jacket and ripped his shirt apart. "Look what the bastard did," he yelled. "Burns all over me. Goddam, that hurts."

Klemm gestured to the two deputies who came in with him. "Take these two out to the cruiser and down to the jail. I'll call the hospital and have somebody come over and look at their burns."

Cooper dropped the hot popcorn kettle on the floor. Breathing hard, he stood exhausted. Sheriff Johnny Klemm looked around at the damage and said, "I'll have old Harmon fix up a bill for the damage and give it to Bilbo. It was his game."

He turned to leave, then turned back and said to Cooper, "When you come in to get the incident reports you can check and see that I spelled your name right."

On the drive to St. Louis, Serena told Cooper that Jimmy Rodriquez was out of the hospital and would be okay when the stitches came out of his face and his two cracked ribs healed. He would not lose his job because Sheriff Johnny Klemm stood up for him over Jack Stadler's objections. Bilbo and Wicker had suffered first degree burns and were out on bond threatening to "Take care of the damn newspaper guy." Sheriff Johnny Klemm told them the next complaint he had against them they were going to state prison.

"Be hard to scare those two," Cooper said.

"You sure did a job on them," Serena said. "You're the talk of the whole county."

"Subscriptions go up?"

"A couple of little old ladies came in wanting to see what the newspaper man looked like."

"What did you tell them?"

"Tall, dark and handsome," she said. "I did admit he couldn't spell very well."

"They didn't need to know that."

The rest of the trip she talked about her family and how they hoped to become U.S. citizens this year. She said she wanted to become a citizen, also, and didn't understand why it was so difficult for them when Muslim kids from a terrorist nation can become citizens almost overnight.

"What if you find out what really happened to your mother and the others and you can't prove it?" she asked, guiding the conversation around to the newspaper and their work.

"That's where I am right now," Cooper said. "That's why we're going to Soldano again. See if Marla Gilbert will tell us anything when I tell her that I know she worked for the FDA on the Soldano case."

"She won't," Serena said. "Why should she? You said all the documentation is missing."

"She doesn't know that. If I can bluff her into thinking we have evidence, which we do with the meat reject paper."

"I don't think we are going to get what we want the conventional way. We'll have to try something different."

"Like what?" Cooper asked.

"I'm thinking. Have you ever read Richard Stark's novels on Parker?"

"No, I don't read many novels."

"Too bad. That's where all the creative thinking is. Parker gets in a jam—he's actually a crook, see—and he helps plan heists. Only something always goes wrong because of the people he works with who aren't all that smart. Parker ends up against the crooks who he helped plan the heist with. He comes up with some devious plans to deal with these people and he doesn't have to follow the law when he does it. I'm going to look back through some Parker novels and see if I can find a plan to adapt to our problem."

"One where we don't have to follow the law?"

"I think you can get by with it if you're dealing with crooks," she said. "And it helps if you're an ex-con." The grin was spread across her face.

"This Parker, does he have some kind of pushy female companion?"

To Serena's surprise, they both got into Marla Gilbert's office. At first she wasn't in, but when Cooper said he wanted to talk about the Stolid project, turned out she was in. Lucky, he thought that he remembered the first name of the project—before correcting himself— the young man, James, had mentioned to him.

Marla was cordial, speaking down slightly to Serena after Cooper introduced her. They got the coffee and Danish treat from Della. Marla was more than nervous, she was almost spastic with her hands fluttering and her speech erratic.

Coffee in one hand, a bearclaw in the other, Cooper said, "Tell me about Stolid, Marla."

"I . . .I don't know what you mean," she said before she dropped her Danish on the floor and spilling her coffee on top of it.

He handed her a copy of the meat reject order the Cluster-mole had given them.

Her hand shook and the paper fluttered.

"John Markham tested the meat. It was radioactive. Soldano's genetic-engineered grain caused this. Now, Markham's dead, but Ellsworth will know. It's bound to come out. You tried to get rid of the FDA records for all this"—waving his hand around the elegant office—"but it's going to come out. I'm going to see that it does. You can't stop it. You did something dishonest and I'm willing to bet you have a hard time going to sleep at night, thinking about what you did. The people you hurt. My mother for one who died with cancer because of what Soldano did. What you did."

"It wasn't the meat, it was the manure they sprayed on her garden," Marla said, her words coming quickly, her eyes tearing up. "You don't know what you're doing. You're going to get us both killed."

"I need you to tell us all about it," Cooper said. "You can put an end to this."

"No, no, I can't. Don't you see, you can't stop this. I can't stop it. You've got to go now."

"Not until you straighten this out, Marla. It's all up to you now. You can save lives and get this off your conscience."

"If you go now, I won't say anything about this to anyone. If I have to call security you'll never go home again."

"That's a threat, Marla."

"Please leave," Marla practically screamed the last word. Within seconds one of the doors in Marla's office opened and the young man, James, stood there. "Anything wrong, Miss Gilbert?" he asked.

"It's all right, James. They're just leaving now." She turned her back on Cooper and Serena and went behind her huge, empty desk. James looked at Cooper and Serena, not leaving, not closing the door.

Serena took Cooper's arm and moved him toward the door they had come through. "Let's go, Cooper. Let's go find Parker."

228

One day before press day. Cooper worked on the wording for his four amazing stories, hog waste dumped in the underground caves, the beating of Jimmy Rodriquez, the killing of the FDA report and cancer causing manure spreading.

He had started all this to salve his conscience for the one time shouting at his mother when he was a child that he hated her. He thought he owed her, that he was obligated to find out everything he could about what had happened to her. His quest had grown to much more, more than he could even have imagined. This was now such a big project he was at the point of not knowing how to handle it. He thought about calling in the *Kansas City Star*, or at least talking with some of the editors he had worked for. However, thinking about it, he wanted the scoop, he wanted the newspaper he now owned to be credited for breaking open the case.

He had to admit, though, he was at a point of knowing, but unable to prove anything. And, up against giant Soldano with their legal and political pull, he was likely to be broken, busted and even end up in prison if he printed what he now knew.

He deleted the last paragraph he had written, looked at the screen, tried a different phraseology without success. When Serena came in he barely noticed her. He had been so engrossed in his composition he hadn't heard her motorcycle.

She patted him on the shoulder as she did each morning, and

went to the coffee pot which was now empty and began preparing another batch. The bag she had brought in with her from McDonald's piqued his appetite and he remembered he hadn't eaten yet. She had the coffee perking and shoved the bag next to his computer.

"You need some Jimmy Dean frozen breakfasts in your freezer," she said. "And you need to buy a workable television."

"I can't stand the commercials," he said. "And those frozen entrees are too hard to chew."

"Ha, ha," she said. "So its needless to ask if you have heard the news this morning."

"New attack on our embassy in the middle east? The President had a news conference saying nothing?"

"Bobby Graham was killed in prison in California," she said.

"Graham's son?" He felt a twinge of compassion. Despite his differences with Graham, this was a disheartening result for the man who had given all his existence and everything he had worked for to save a son who had gone astray.

"I knew him," she said. "He had friends at our school, older than me, but we were acquainted. Small towns, you know. Bobby was always kind of different. Everyone liked him though. I'm sorry for Mister Graham. He's not a bad man."

"Tomorrow remind me to call him. He's going to need help with his newspaper."

"He might skip a day and not publish," Serena said.

"No, he's a newspaper man first, even taking precedence over being a father. He'll publish something."

"We'll see about five o'clock," she said. "That's when it gets delivered."

THE CLUSTER COUNTY CARRIER

THE EDITOR'S FINAL SAY TO HIS READERS

The Constitution of the United States and all the men and women who have died defending and protecting it have given me the right and duty to write my last article for *The Cluster Carrier*. I can only hope that the good and decent people in this county and in this state will take what I say in this article and do the right thing. As I should have done from the beginning.

Seven years ago the Soldano Agricultural Corporation began an experiment on their seeds with the intent and desire to increase corporate profits. A program called STOLID was initiated in which common grain seeds were treated in such a manner that the harvested seeds when fed to livestock would increase their body weight double that of ordinary grains. The method of treatment was known only to executives of Soldano. The FDA did not know nor did the workers who worked in the super secret project. What the company needed was animals to test the harvested grain on. The animal which responded the best to the new grain was the pig. A lot of pigs were needed so the idea of a massive hog farm was introduced by a stockholder in Soldano named Jack Stadler. The same Jack Stadler who is and has been for forty years, the Cluster County Assessor. By hook or by crook, Stadler had become the owner of 2400 acres of farm land in our county. Soldano decided Stadler had a good idea so they began plans for the massive hog operation.

Standing in the way of the hog farm was the state environmental officer Martin Dinsmore. He was paid handsomely to pass a report of acceptability to the Farm Services Agency who had the final say on a permit for the hog farm. It is unclear at this point how the federal agency, Environmental Protection Agency was bypassed. Grady Quichen, the Farm Services Agent for Cluster County was rewarded with a waiver on county and state taxes.

A slight hitch in the plans for expansion of the hog farm was three pieces of property surrounded by Stadler's 2400 acres. Grant Borden, Lou Magliole and Cecilia Roth owned small acreage properties. They all refused to sell to Soldano, although the offers were quite handsome. When the farm became operational, the odor that came from it was close to unbearable to those three property owners. They complained to the sheriff, to the county commissioners and to the *Cluster County Carrier*. Stadler got to all of us. Nothing was done. The 2400 acres and the three properties were atop a series of underground caves that spelunkers from all over the state frequented, naming them as some of the best challenges in caves in the cave state. Before long, those spelunkers started complaining about the smell in the caves. The smell of hog manure. They felt the hog farm was dumping the hog waste into the underground caverns. All the cavers were denied access to the caves except through the three properties. These three land owners had been charging admission to the caves for some time for a modest income. There was something else being discovered in the caves according to one man who had entered with a Geiger counter. The caves were now radioactive.

Something else was happening on the hog farm. Though the hogs were gaining weight rapidly—doubling their weight over a few days—the hogs were dying prematurely and people who ate the pork products from the hogs were getting sick. Thousands of pounds of pork was being processed on the farm without a market. Arrowhead Trucking was busy hauling in material used at Soldano in treating the grain seeds and hauling out pork products to be shipped to China and other countries outside the U.S. The owners of the three surrounded properties became sick, whether from the radioactive material now being dumped in the caves, the liquified manure spread on their gardens or by eating the pork products. Reports of cancer increased in Cluster County and in surrounding counties where the pork products were marketed on a trial basis. The three land owners ended up getting killed. Cody Wicker and Edward Bilbo were paid by Jurgen Miehle, son of Everett Miehle who, along with his brother were owners of controlling interest in Soldano, to get rid of the three property owners. They were all murdered. Four other murders have occurred including Martin Dinsmore who had resigned from the state environmental office to a mansion in Florida, but who mistakenly returned for another reward after his property was foreclosed on.

There is no record of STOLID in Soldano's corporate papers. There is no record with the FDA that such a project ever existed. The FDA agent in charge of Soldano's experiments was Marla Gilbert who now works for Everett Miehle. Jared Carson, Miehle's attorney, arranged payments to J.S. Larned, president of Home Bank in New Port. Larned in turn transferred the payment amounts to Stadler who doled the money out to his courthouse cronies.

There is no proof of any of what I have written. There is no smoking gun. I have told you what happened. I know because I was part of it. I've been a journalist all my life, it's in my blood. I regret I did not stop this when I might have been able to. I placed my life and that of those close to me over your life. But, as a lifelong observer, I took note of what was going on. This is what I noted. The rest is up to you.

The Special Edition

Cooper closed the paper. Serena, who had already read the article before giving it to Cooper, said, "He did what you wanted to do. They're going to sue his ass off."

"I need to call him," Cooper said. Serena did the dialing, he listened to the phone's busy signal. "He's getting a lot of calls. Can't get through this way. I'm driving there, we need to talk."

The office of the *Cluster County Carrier* was cordoned off with yellow crime scene tape. Cooper ducked under the tape and was stopped by a deputy before he got to the door.

"What's going on?" Cooper asked.

"Sir, this is off limits to the public. You'll have to leave."

"I'm Cooper Rease, the *Special Edition*. I need to talk with Mister Graham or the sheriff."

"Not possible, sir. If you'll step back outside the tape . . . "

Sheriff Johnny Klemm appeared in the doorway. "It's all right, Brad. Let Rease inside."

Cooper came through the door to find Klemm and two other deputies inside. The swivel chair Graham usually sat in was covered with blood.

"My God, what happened?" He asked the sheriff.

"According to the people who work here, they came in this morning and found Graham in the chair dead. He had a gunshot wound in the head and a pistol on the floor where he had apparently dropped it."

"You think he shot himself?"

"It appears that way," the sheriff said. "The woman who came in first usually found the door unlocked as Graham beat her in each day. This morning she found the door locked and had to wait until the press men came in with a key. Apparently Graham had stayed up all night and ran the paper off by himself."

"After he heard his son was dead." Cooper said. "Where's Bilbo and Wicker? Are we sure they weren't involved?"

"They're out on bail, but not until two o'clock this afternoon. He was already dead by then."

"Hard to believe he put the paper out by himself," Cooper said. "He labeled it and took it to the post office. Quite a job. I know, I do our's and I have excellent help."

Sheriff Johnny Klemm said, "You didn't by chance come by to help him?"

"Me? No, of course not. What makes you think that?"

"Didn't. Just asking to make sure, though. He left an envelope addressed to you."

"To me?"

Klemm handed him a sealed manilla envelope with Cooper Rease written on the outside. "I could hold it for evidence," he said.

"Meaning you would like to see what's inside?"

"Might be helpful."

Cooper opened the envelope and took out a folded one-sheet note with a check inside. The check was made out to him for twenty-five thousand dollars. The note said "Finish the job." Graham had signed his name.

29

Cooper told Serena to meet him at the courthouse. The sun had dipped below the horizon when she showed up and he took his eyes off a colorful layering of blazing-edged clouds that faded from bright magenta to cool lemon.

He took her to Sheriff Johnny Klemm's office and showed her the papers they had taken from Graham's office. Most of them consisted of notes Graham had made about the people in the courthouse, about the hog farm and about the murders.

"No proof," he told her, "but he connects the dots, especially the ones we couldn't connect. They're a road map telling us how to get the proof."

"Yeah," she said. "But Soldano holds the proof. They won't let go of it without a fight."

"I'm ready for a fight. So are you. We're going to get the proof. Graham laid it out, we're going to finish it."

Sheriff Johnny Klemm said, "At least you know what you're up against. I need some warrants before I can do any more investigating. And Judge Harold Turner doesn't sign warrants with the name Soldano on them."

"Then we'll go around the judge," Cooper said.

"Good luck with that," the sheriff said.

Before getting back on her Triumph she told Cooper she thought she saw one of Bilbo's cars in the lot at the Broken Bow.

Cooper climbed on the back of her cycle. "Let's take a look."

He put his hands around her waist, liking the feel of her tiny body, and leaned forward to say, "Take it easy, don't throw me off."

She cruised well within the speed limit, past the closed businesses, past the darkened office of the *Cluster County Carrier*—the yellow tape taken down—and on out of town to the ramshackle Broken Bow roadhouse.

Seven cars were in the lot at this time of night. Serena rode slowly around the lot closest to the road so it would be difficult to be seen. She pointed her finger at a gleaming sedan Cooper recognized as a Bentley. Definitely Bilbo's automobile. No one else in Cluster County drove a Bentley. Or any county close to them.

She turned back onto the highway, headed back to the courthouse where Cooper had left his Toyota. Reluctantly he dismounted.

"Take it easy going home," he said. "I'll be right behind you."

She nodded and eased away. He watched her until she turned the corner back onto the highway to New Port. He walked toward the Toyota, noticing the sheriff's office was now dark. No deputies on night duty. As he got into the Toyota and closed the door he saw headlights go by driving fast. He looked at the car and his pulse jumped.

The car was a Bentley.

He would never have found her if his headlights hadn't reflected off her helmet lying in the weeds alongside the road. He wheeled the Toyota off the road, jammed it in PARK and ran across the road, down an embankment, past the motorcycle lying on its side, yelling now, looking right and left, then he saw her. Her little body was sprawled on the ground and he could tell she had been hurt badly.

He ran to her, kneeled beside her, lifted her head and saw the stream of blood trickling out of her mouth. He tried to remember the precautions given for moving an injured person, but couldn't. He heard himself talking, yelling even. He held her head in one hand, the other smoothing her forehead. He was talking nonsense. Before he knew it, before he could remember the precautions, he had her in his arms carrying her up the incline.

He calmed somewhat as he dropped to his knees. He laid her on the ground and her head rolled to the side, limply.

"Oh, God," he cried out. "Don't let this happen, God. Please, God, please."

His agony was so deep he thought he would pass out. No, he couldn't. She depended on him, he had to stay calm. He had his cell phone in his hand punching in 9-1-1. He told the operator he needed an ambulance immediately and Sheriff Johnny Klemm. He was told the only available ambulance would be there in about thirty minutes. The operator kept asking him questions: what was his name, where was his location, who was injured, how was the person injured.

He put the phone in his pocket and stood up. Do the right thing, his mind told him. Her life is your life now.

But what to do? He knew he couldn't wait thirty minutes. He knelt and felt her pulse. Weak, but still beating. He ran to the Toyota, opened the back door, ran back to Serena, picked her up, put her in the back seat, closed the door, got in and started off, jamming his foot into the accelerator, headed for the hospital.

He had to be in time. He just had to be. Right now that was the most important thing in the world to him. On the way to the hospital his thoughts rambled, but finally a vow formed in his mind. Bilbo and Cody Wicker were done in this county. Forever.

30

Daylight was breaking. He stared at the television on the wall in the waiting room. An infomercial was playing about a wonder pan for cooking, but his mind didn't pick it up. The empty paper coffee cup sat on the table in front of him. Nothing was on his mind. It was numb. Fernando and Rosalind Gonzalez sat across from him on the sofa. Their faces showed no emotion, but he knew how they must feel. He knew they must be holding him at cause for what had happened to their daughter.

He had called them on the way to the hospital and they were there waiting for him to arrive as was a gurney to take Serena inside. He told them she had been run off the highway by Edward Bilbo and Cody Wicker, though he lacked any evidence other than to see them driving after her.

Sheriff Johnny Klemm found him in the waiting room. He listened as Cooper explained what he knew and what he suspected.

"Judge should never have let them out," the sheriff said. "I'll drive by the Broken Bow, Bilbo's car lot and his house. If I don't find them tonight, I will tomorrow. You say the car was a Bentley? That's one of those fancy English cars isn't it? I'll check it for scratches."

The sheriff expressed his concern to the Gonzalezes before leaving. Cooper wanted to say more to Serena's parents, but he was finding it awkward. They had to be thinking if he hadn't called her to come to the courthouse tonight when she wasn't even supposed to be working, she wouldn't be lying on the operating table. And dying—but he couldn't think of her dying. She couldn't die, he wouldn't let her. God wouldn't let her.

A nurse occasionally passed by the window in the room looking out on the hallway and his eyes followed her. Then his thoughts went back to the small, young woman he was forced to leave in the operating room by the attending physician. An accident on the other side of the town had brought the surgeon in to attend to the injuries of a teenage boy who had gone to sleep, ran his father's pickup into a tree and suffered a head injury. The boy had been removed to a recovery room minutes before Cooper had driven up to the emergency room door with Serena.

Another cup of instant coffee, another trip into the hallway looking toward the IC unit where one of the nurses told him Serena would be taken after surgery. He saw no one.

He had just dozed off for no more than a minute when the surgeon entered the waiting room still in his stained white gown and the head cover. He removed his gloves, held them in one hand.

"She's unconscious, but stable," he said to the parents. "She's had a concussion, but we didn't find any damage to the brain. She has a broken left arm which will heal and some contusions to her body and one leg. None of the injuries seem to be life threatening, except we can't predict about the coma."

The doctor said he was remaining at the hospital to follow her condition and the Gonzalezes thanked him. When he left, Fernando and Rosalind urged Cooper to get something to eat and to go home and rest for a couple of hours. They promised to call him. But he couldn't leave.

"I feel responsible," he said. "I care a great deal for her. I can't leave until I know she'll be all right."

"Don't take it on yourself," Rosalind told him. "You have no idea what a good effect you have had on her. Going to work for you has been the best thing in her life."

Fernando was nodding his head in agreement, but Cooper said, "Look what it's gotten her. I never wanted anyone else to be hurt. If it had been me, that would have been different. They must have seen both of us on her motorcycle and meant to kill us both. They're going to pay for this. The newspaper and all the other deaths don't mean anything today. Only her."

"Get something to eat," Fernando said. "Come back and we'll take turns waiting for her to wake up. You're more tired than us, you go first."

Cooper wasn't sure he could eat anything. He was afraid to go to sleep again. What if something happened while he was asleep and he never saw her again.

He went to the cafeteria, ordered some breakfast, ate a few bites, drank some real coffee—dark and strong, and headed back to the waiting room. The Gonzalezes were still sitting sternly on the sofa. He urged them to go to the cafeteria and reluctantly they did. Before they returned Sheriff Johnny Klemm came back. He hadn't located Bilbo and Wicker, but he had taken a warrant to Judge Turner who refused to sign it.

"There's got to be some changes in this county," he said. He looked hard at Cooper as if charging him with the task of forcing the changes.

At least, that's how Cooper felt so he assumed the sheriff felt the same.

The day passed slowly. The newspaper creeped back into Cooper's thoughts. They had gotten this week's issue out with the four stories Cooper wanted to tell, somewhat diluted compared to Graham's last issue of the *Carrier*. The thought occurred to Cooper that getting next week's issue out was going to be very difficult without Serena and the pain once again of her condition agonized him.

Graham had laid it out for him. He printed his expose, knowing it would be his last and knowing Soldano couldn't do anything about it. They owned Graham's paper so who were they going to sue for libel? Themselves? Graham left him the challenge to provide the proof that would unravel the whole Soldano scheme. But how he was going to do it was unclear. After what they did to Serena he was even more determined to destroy their operation. Serena had provided him with the solution when she talked about the fictional character Parker in Richard Stark's—actually Donald Westlake's—books. The next day he decided she was right and he resolved to take action.

Early in the evening, after the Gonzalezes retuned from a nearby restaurant, the head nurse came in the waiting room to tell them they could see their daughter. Cooper waited anxiously to see if they would find her awake, perhaps, or at least improved. They did not. Trying to be cheerful, they, nevertheless transmitted to him their deepening concern. To his inquiry, the nurse informed him he would have to wait to see Serena. Two visits close together might be too taxing. Something he didn't understand since Serena would not know he was there.

Nightfall brought the surgeon who had treated Serena to the waiting room. He expressed some hope for the parents and for Cooper who expressed his great desire to see her. Both Fernando and Rosalind told the doctor they thought he should let Cooper visit their daughter.

"For five minutes, only," the doctor said. "I'm somewhat concerned that her pulse rate has declined throughout the day. I'm not sure what's causing that."

The sight of her as he entered the all white room was disconcerting. Such a vital person, so full of life, so capable to be completely stilled and looking as if she was no longer of this world. He noticed the cycling of her heartbeat on the electrocardiograph, the lowered reading of blood pressure, and other indications signaled by the instrument faces above her bed.

He began talking to her as if they were sitting facing each other in their makeshift office in the mobile home. He told her they got the paper out on time, that she would have to hurry up and get well so she could help him get the next issue out.

Her face nor the instruments gave any indication she heard anything he said and he realized the foolishness of his one-way conversation. "Listen," he told her. "I need you. You've got to get better. I can't do this without you. You're more a part of the newspaper than I am. You're the one keeping it going."

He wasn't saying what he really felt. He was holding back.

"Dammit, little brown girl, don't you see? Don't you know by now? You've got to get well. Because . . . because, well, you know . . . " He wiped his cheek with the back of his wrist and it came away wet. "I love you, Serena, didn't you know that? Please get well."

The electrocardiograph raced, reaching higher peaks. The pulse rate, the blood pressure soared. The closed eyelids flickered and one tear rolled down her cheek.

He breathed in the night air and it felt good. Everything felt better. She would live, he knew that now. After his visit, after the doctor checked on her after Cooper told him about her reaction, the prognosis was encouraging. The Gonzalezes were relieved and smiles appeared on their faces. Cooper needed to get outside, out where the elation inside him could expand, soar and free him from the deep despair where he had been since he had found her by the side of the road. He got in the Toyota and decided to make a quick trip to the mobile home, shower, change clothes, have one beer and some chips, cheese and salsa.

He began planning how he was going to fix up the mobile home. When he had offered the check from Graham to the Gonzalezes, they insisted he keep the money as a loan to get an office—"For when she gets well," they said.

He drove by Bilbo's car lot and saw a light in his sales office. Anger surged through him and he braked the Toyota to the curb. He took the tire iron from the trunk and walked back along the street to the car lot. He angled through the cars in front coming up on the lighted office from the side which blocked their vision. At the front he saw Bilbo and Cody Wicker sitting at the sales desk facing each other. He tried the latch, found it unlocked, opened the door quickly advancing on the two as they sat at the desk. He saw at once they both had a pistol in front of them on the desk and he took two quick strides toward Bilbo raising the tire iron as he did. Neither of them looked up as he prepared to strike. That was when he noticed Bilbo had a small round hole in the middle of his forehead. He glanced at Wicker and saw that he too had a similar hole between his eyes. When Cooper nudged the desk with his leg, both the heads of Bilbo and Cody Wicker dropped with a thud onto the desktop.

Dead!

CHOICES

"We don't get to chose what is true. We only get to choose what we do about it."
 —Author Kami Garcia, *Beautiful Darkness*

The tall man dressed in black walked under the sign that read BILBO'S EXCLUSIVE USED CARS and walked toward the sales office. He looked at the automobiles as he passed them— exclusive, all of them, English, German, Swedish, Italian—and by appearance he was a man who could afford any of them. He had about him a certain jauntiness and sophistication that would match well with imports.

Bilbo saw him coming and dashed out of the office to greet him. The man was cordial and smiled back at Bilbo and his sales pitch. When Bilbo got down to the generic used car pitch of, "What did you have in mind," the man suggested they go in the office and discuss his specific desires.

Cody Wicker sat at the sales desk, a nail file in a manicured hand. He nodded and Bilbo introduced Wicker as an assistant and that brought a sneer to his face. The man set his briefcase on the desk and said, "Now, let's get serious." He extracted an iPad from the briefcase, hit a few keys and turned it around to face Bilbo. The camera eye blinked red.

"What we're going to do here and how this is going to go is you will go first, Mister Bilbo, and you will look at the camera and tell us exactly how you murdered seven people and who paid you to do it."

Wicker became motionless and Bilbo looked as if he had been struck with a heavy object.

"Who the hell are you?" he managed to get out. His face had lost color and his long, pompadoured, blonde hair fell limply across one eye. Wicker's face, by contrast, turned bright red. His right hand slid smoothly off the table toward the holster on his hip.

The man looked at Wicker and said with one hand still in his briefcase, "What's going to happen if your hand comes up with a pistol in it I will kill you before you can use it."

Wicker's hand stopped moving as Bilbo repeated, "Who the hell are you?"

"I'm the man who's going to take your confession," the man told him.

"The hell you are. I don't know what the hell you're talking about. You're crazy if you think I'm going to confess to something I never did."

"You were involved. You and your friend here. After your confession we'll know who did the killing, won't we?"

"You crazy bastard . . . " Bilbo said and the man's free hand pointed at Bilbo and an electrical charge snapped across the space between them and Bilbo froze, his eyes bugged and he shook like a wet dog.

"They call it a friendly tazer," the man said in a calm voice. "Lesser charge, but unpleasant nevertheless. Shall we get started with the confession?"

Bilbo's mouth was moving without words coming out. The man said, "We'll wait for you to regain your composure."

Wicker started to rise and the man pointed his hand toward him and when the charge hit him Wicker shuddered and grabbed the edge of the table. The man turned back to Bilbo. "Let's get started," he said.

Bilbo's eyes threatened to come out of his head. "I . . .I . . . don't know . . . I didn't . . ."

The man said, his voice still calm, "How many times are we going to have to do this?"

"I'll . . .say . . . whatever . . . you want . . ."

"You know what I want. Let's start with Grant Borden. You dynamited his place and shot him in the head twice. Tell me about that."

"It was Cody there . . ."

Wicker shouted, "Bilbo shut your goddamn mouth you crazy son of a bitch."

The man gave Wicker another zap from his left hand and Wicker tripped on his chair and fell writhing to the floor.

Bilbo began blabbering, not putting words in the proper order to make any sense. The man pointed his left hand at him and Bilbo screamed out, "No, no. I'll talk. Don't do it again."

The man waited. Bilbo wiped saliva from his mouth and chin. Wicker sat on the floor, shaking viciously, still for a moment then shaking again.

Bilbo told how they were sent to Grant Borden's farm, tried to get him to sign a bill of sale for his property, tied him to a chair, set the stick of dynamite under his chair and lit the fuse. Borden then agreed to sign, they untied him and Borden then tore up the paper so Wicker shot him. When he didn't die right away, he shot him again in a fit of anger and told Bilbo to blow the place up.

Wicker, by this time had stopped his violent shaking and sat staring hard at Bilbo in silence.

Bilbo went on to how they killed Lou Magliole, Elsie Loring

and Jose Rodriquez."

"How about the other three?" the man asked.

"No, no. Jurgen did the rest. We didn't have anything to do with them."

"Who paid you to do all this?"

"Jurgen. We got an interest in the hog farm and ten thousand apiece."

"That's good," the man said. He turned the iPad around to face Wicker, still on the floor. "Now let's hear you confirm what your compatriot told me."

"Go to hell," Wicker said, his eyes slitted like a cat.

"Oh, well, be stubborn then. Bilbo might get life instead of the big sleep. Now, here's what's going to happen next." He took two pistols from the briefcase and laid them on opposite sides of the table. "Each pistol has one cartridge in it. You two can face each other and I'm going to be waiting outside. The first one out the door can get in the Bentley there and head for Mexico if that's your desire. If the other one comes out behind him, I'll have to shoot him. Okay, you understand what you're to do, right?"

Bilbo looked at the pistol on the table in front of him. He nodded his head vigorously. Wicker, sitting on the floor, said, "Go to hell."

The man brought a black automatic from the briefcase and said to Wicker, "Get rid of the pistol on your hip, there."

"Go to hell."

The man's automatic fired and Wicker jerked and slapped a hand to his side where the holster and pistol were. "Goddam," he said.

"Get rid of the pistol."

Wicker, grimacing, took the pistol out of the holster, looked at the man, thought about it, then skidded it across the floor.

"Now," the man said, "take a seat at the table."

Bilbo quickly sat down, licked his lips, looked at the pistol in front of him, looked at Wicker, then at the man. Wicker took a seat across from him, placed a hand on the table inches away from the pistol.

The man backed his way to the door, briefcase in one hand, the automatic in the other. "The best chance you have is to be the first one out the door," he said. "Oh, yes, just to hurry things along, this grenade has a ten second fuse on it."

He took a round metallic object from the briefcase and rolled it under the table and he was gone out the door.

He waited outside, heard two shots go off almost simultaneously, then a pop like from the M-80 firecracker he'd rolled under the table.

The man looked back through the door and saw both men sitting at the desk facing each other. The pistols had fallen onto the table. He walked to the Bentley, got in and drove away.

32

J. S. Larkin walked past the receptionist outside his office at the Home Bank in New Port as she was trying to tell him something. He entered the office of the president, his office, and saw a tall man in work coveralls and a cap. The receptionist caught up with him then and said, "I was trying to say, Mister Larkin, he's here with your new chair."

"What new chair," Larkin said. "I didn't order a new chair."

The tall man said with a grin, "Here's the order for a new chair for the Man of The Year from the Chamber of Commerce."

"What?" Larkin said, looked at the handsome, rich leather tufted chair—much more executive appearing than his own. "No one said anything to me about a new chair. Or Man of The Year."

The man shrugged. "Well, they did say something about it being a surprise. I think they didn't expect you to return so soon. Sit down, try it out."

The phone in the outer office sounded then and the receptionist backed out of the office and closed the door. Larkin looked at the chair, ran his hand over the leather and sat in it.

"Don't bounce up and down," the man told him. "It's armed now."

"What?" Larkin asked, bewildered.

"Don't bounce up and down in it. Most of all, don't get up.

You see, it has a slab of plastic explosive in the seat. When you sat down you armed it."

"What are you saying?" Larkin paled and his mustache quivered.

"I'm saying I put an explosive in your new chair. If you raise up your asshole will be up there on the ceiling."

"What the hell . . ."

"See, here's what's going to happen. You have a request on your computer to download all the payments made to you personally at the bank here and to all the transfers of those payments to Jack Stadler, the county assessor. All I need is your signature on that order and those records will be transferred to my iPad. Here is the scroll pad I'm going to plug into your USB port and you will use the digital pen to sign the order."

"I don't know what the hell you're talking about," Larkin said, the words exploding from his mouth. "You can't walk into this bank and order me to do anything."

"See, after you've signed the order and the records have been transferred, I'll be leaving. You will remain seated for the next hour at which time I will e-mail directions to your secretary on how to disarm the charge in your chair. You could, of course, call the police when I leave, in which case I will not send the directions and it's very doubtful the police will be able to figure out how to disarm the chair. They can try, but if they fail, BOOM"

"Who are you?"

"Call me the competition. I have an interest in this."

"You can't get away with this."

"Perhaps not. But then, neither can you."

The man took a silver scroll pad from his case, attached it to Larkin's desktop computer and handed Larkin the digital pen.

"Hell, I sign this it's like a confession to illegal money transfers," Larkin said, his voice starting to plead.

The man shrugged. "You have a choice, of course. I could just leave."

Larkin's hand holding the digital pen, shook. The man said, "Make it authentic, I can detect any difference between what you sign and your regular signature."

Larkin looked at the scroll pad as if it was a pan of fire that he was supposed to thrust his hand into. Slowly, he signed his name with the pen.

"Good," the man said. "That's good."

The man entered a command in Larkin's computer and waited, then smiled. "Done," he said. "I'll be on my way. Remember, one hour."

The man left the office, waved at the receptionist on his way out the door and down the street to a parked Bentley at the curb. He drove away. An hour passed and he looked at the clock and smiled, speeding up slightly, then tuned the radio to a classical music station.

333

Marla Gilbert walked into her spacious office, set her Michael Kors Himalayan goatskin leather purse on her shining fifteen foot long desk and walked around it to her pink leather reclining executive chair before she saw the man. He appeared to be someone who belonged in the main offices of Soldano. He was dark haired, handsome and expensively dressed. He smiled at her, but she couldn't muster a smile in return. Anything or anyone unfamiliar or unplanned in advance frightened Marla.

"Marla,'" he said, rising to come forward and stand before her, "we have some business to conduct, in a pleasant way, of course."

"What . . .what business?" Marla asked, trepidation rising inside. "I don't know you. How did you get in here?"

He handed a card to her, but she didn't take it, only stared at his hand, then his face.

"You seem a bit unsure about this," he said, "so let's get it over with. You have in a safety deposit box under the name of Morgan Sneed—that was your grandfather's name on your mother's side, wasn't it?—clever to use it, a name you wouldn't forget. In the box is the whole FDA file on Soldano's project STOLID which ended up in disaster after John Markham's lab test. You of course had the whole file expunged, a deed you exchanged for all this, some Soldano stock and a handsome salary.

Public be damned. Now, what I want from you is that file. The file Ev Miehle knows you have and will use against Soldano if your terms to him aren't met."

"I don't know what you're talking about," Marla said, white-faced and shaking.

"Don't blame you for denying it," the man said. "I would do the same if I'd done such a dishonorable deed. Nevertheless, here's what you're to do. Go to Central Bank and open the safety deposit box, take out the file, walk out onto the street where you will see a man in a black Bentley sedan parked. Give the file to that man and you will be free to go."

"You're crazy," Marla shrieked. "Even if there was such a file, why would I give it to you?"

"You don't have to, of course. You have choices. One, you could call security and have me escorted from the building. In which case I would let Ev Miehle know where the file is and under what name. You can figure out who you would rather have the file, me or Ev Miehle. Choice number two you could chose to do nothing. Ignore me completely and get on with your life. In which case I would let Jurgen think that I had the file and he would then assume you were no longer necessary to the company. That would work for me because you have a trust set up with an attorney in Milwaukee that in case of violent death or suicide the file would go to the head of the FDA. Which is where I plan to send it myself."

"You're crazy," Marla repeated.

"Or choice number three which I spelled out for you in the beginning. Which is it to be?"

"I can't do that." She began to cry. "The file is released and I'm dead."

The Special Edition

"Or, if you take choice number three, there's Mexico. Or, on your handsome rewards you got from Soldano, there's the Riviera or a number of nice, lonely places. You could, of course, throw yourself on the mercy of the court, confess your sins and pray for forgiveness and a suspended sentence. Choices, choices."

"What . . .what time will the car be at the bank?"

Marla's shoes made a clacking sound on the marble floor and she cursed herself for wearing shoes with a hard leather heel. She walked quieter on the toes of her shoes to the desk where people wanting to access their safety deposit box registered. She exchanged greetings to the woman at the desk, signed her name as Morgan Sneed, produced a photo identification for that name and handed her box key to the woman. Inside the secure room the woman left her alone. With trembling hands she opened the large drawer and took out the plastic briefcase holding nearly a thousand pages of official papers with the Food and Drug Administration line at the bottom of each sheet. Despite knowing she was alone, she glanced around surreptitiously. She replaced the empty drawer and signed out at the woman's desk.

"I've got to make a call if you don't mind," she told the woman as she extracted her phone from the expensive purse, pressed in a number and when a voice answered, she said, "I'm coming out."

She walked into the main lobby, the heels clacking again, and headed for the front door. Stepping from behind the end of the teller's counter the man who had been in her office took her arm.

"I'll take the case now, Marla. You fooled me calling the FDA who sent the FBI agent over. He can arrest the man I hired to sit in the Bentley, but the man knows nothing. You can, of course, tell the security man over there by the door with a gun that I'm robbing you or molesting you or something. In which case, I would be arrested and the FBI would get the file and who knows what would happen after that."

Marla was speechless. The man took the file and said to her, "My advice? Find a place with sunny beaches and no extradition agreement with the U.S. Oh, and here, give this fifty dollar bill to the young man in the Bentley and ask him to drive it back to the shopping mall and leave it in the parking lot. And the keys under the mat."

Marla at last realized her mouth was gaping open as she closed it with a snap.

The Bentley was where it was supposed to be. He spotted the first of them sitting by the window inside a coffee shop looking obviously out of place. Another one sat in a black, four-door Chevrolet two spaces from the Bentley trying to look inconspicuous behind an unfolded newspaper. The man knew there would only be two of them for this job. He approached the Chevrolet and tapped on the window. The sandy-haired man inside looked up from his newspaper. The tall man held a card up to the window and waited while the man inside read it, looked out again, back to the photo ID and nodded. The man outside motioned for the window to be lowered. Through the opening he said, "I'm taking the Bentley. Any problems?"

A glance again at the card held up to him and the sandy-haired agent shook his head.

The Special Edition

"Tell you friend in the coffee shop," he was told. He nodded and the man standing outside the Chevrolet put the card back in his pocket, threw a salute to the agent inside and walked to the Bentley and drove away.

The sandy-haired agent pulled his phone from a pocket, slid his finger to a number and tapped, waited, then said, "Terminate."

"

Lisa Allen sat at her usual position at the bar, leaving one seat empty between her and the end where the polished mahogany top curved around. Her friend would join her in about a half an hour and, unless something developed by way of the empty stool, she would join her friend at their usual table. She ordered what she always ordered, barely spiked fruit-flavored drink that not only looked delicious, but tasted so as well. And the bit of gin—the exact amount the bartender knew by now how much to add—to give her just the right amount of buzz. Relaxation she needed after a day of compiling phony press releases the group she headed created for the area's largest corporation.

A man slid onto the stool she had purposely left vacant. Without turning to directly engage him, she could tell he was going to be quite handsome, fiftyish maybe—younger would be more desirable, but wouldn't have the money or power the older ones have. When he said, "Hello there, Lisa," she turned quickly to see a man, handsome indeed and quite prosperous looking, but unfamiliar. She smiled while trying to place him and could not. The man gave an order to the bartender and said to replenish Lisa's drink. She didn't object.

While the bartender put the order together, she said to the man, "I'm sure we've met, but I'm not recalling where."

"Perhaps not in person," he said, taking the drink the bartender set in front of him and lifting it in a proposed toast, "but I know you quite well, Lisa, and I'm impressed by you."

Courteously, she lifted her glass in a half-salute, took a sip and gave the man her look over the glass as she had done many times. "And how would that be?" she asked.

He brought one of those smart phones out, tapped it and held it up for her to see. The video that had been taken in one of her encounters with Jurgen was playing on the screen of the smart phone and she was speechless. Her face burned and she looked around to see if anyone in the bar, practically empty at this time of day, could also see the smart phone's screen.

"Where did you get that?" she finally got out.

"You had a whole drawer full of them," the man said, smiling. It wasn't a smile like he was coming on to her, more of a smile like he'd caught her doing something she shouldn't have been doing. Who the hell was this guy?

"You broke into my apartment?"

"This is all I took, honest. Well, to be truthful I took them all. Eleven to be exact. I haven't looked at all of them, of course."

"What do you want?" the anger now replaced by a rising sense of dread.

"Easy," the man still talking smooth like maybe he really was coming on to her, only she knew he wasn't, "I just want you to make a call."

"A call?"

"Yes. To Jurgen."

"Jurgen?"

"Correct. I want you to tell him to meet you at the cave on the farm. The one where you shot the video. That you're dying to make another."

"Another video?"

"Oh, you won't have to meet him, I'll do that. But you, with your charm and sensual abilities can entice him to meet me. You don't mention that, of course. Just say what I ask you to say."

"Who are you? What do you want with Jurgen?"

"Just want to talk with him. And I'm nobody. Tomorrow you will have forgotten you even met me."

"Why would I do this?"

"Well, I was thinking these videos would look great on that porno youTube type of site. You know the one? You could have a future there if you really wanted a career change, you know. I might be doing you a favor. But, then, I'll bet the company you work for and the people you work with would get a charge out of watching them, also. I'll bet this would go viral in no time. It's better than a cat playing the piano."

"You're putting my private videos on the internet?"

"Either that or, after you make that call to Jurgen, I'm mailing them back to you. You can trust me, I'm not really a fan of these. Too personal."

Lisa looked at the bartender who looked at her tall, fluted glass, saw it was still full and turned his attention to another customer. She tried to reason it all out. "He'll be pissed at me if I set him up like you want," she said. "He hurts people."

"Not anymore. See, I've got a few embarrassing items of Jurgen's that will make him forget all about your phone call."

"You're going to kill him, aren't you?"

"No, no. Not me. I try not to hurt people. Physically, I mean. Nasty business that. I just like to give people choices. You have two choices, you call him or you don't."

She took a drink of her personal concoction she had worked

out, but it didn't taste as good as usual. She set it back on the bar. "What do you want me to say?" she asked the man.

35

Jurgen stepped out of his BMW coupe in front of the limestone shrouded entrance to the cave now blocked by a wrought iron gate with a lock on it. He glanced over at the black Bentley sedan with dark windows he couldn't see through. Puzzling was how Lisa got an expensive automobile that she told him she would be driving.

He wore a $120 maroon T-shirt he rad ripped the sleeves from. Tats ran off his shoulder to his elbows of ferocious cage fighters that his father had lectured him about. "How the hell you going to look in a boardroom when you take over for me with those goddam tattoos all over you?"

Little did the old man know that by the time he took over the boardroom, everyone at the table would have tats under their shirt, even the women. Hell, especially the women.

He reached inside the Beamer and tooted the horn one time. What the hell was she waiting for. He went over to open the door of the Bentley, but a tall man, taller even than Jurgen and as well built, well dressed, but what? fiftyish? got out. Jurgen stopped, looked the guy over, wondered who the hell he was and where was the sexy bitch Lisa.

"Jurgen," the man said, a friendly smile on his face, "how you doing?"

"Who the hell are you?" Jurgen asked.

The Special Edition

The man, getting used to that same question from everyone, said, "I'm the game changer, Jurgen. That's the new buzz words, right?"

"What frigging game you talking about?"

"This game, the hog farm, Soldano. Killing women and old men."

Jurgen propped both hands on his hips, looked closer at the guy. Did he have a gun? He could take the guy easy. "I don't know who you are, buddy, but you're getting ready to get your ass kicked."

"I'm the guy who's going to give you some choices, Jurgen. Get you to make some executive decisions. Son of a powerful man, you ought to be capable of making some big decisions."

"I've decided I've had enough of you," Jurgen said, stepped forward to take hold of the man's arm when something electric ran through him, rattling every nerve in his body and burning his face and eyes and ringing his ears. And the son of a bitch was just standing there smiling at him, his finger pointing at him.

"What I want you to do now, Jurgen, is come over here and crawl inside the trunk of the Bentley. It's a nice trunk, you'll be comfortable."

Jurgen couldn't answer. His skin was still tingling and felt like it was on fire. The man took him by the arm and led him over to the Bentley, opened the trunk and the next thing Jurgen knew he was on his back lying in the trunk of the damn car, his knees all doubled up.

He felt the automobile moving and he fought the feeling of vomiting, closed his eyes and tried to reason what had happened to him and how the hell the man had done whatever it was he did.

The man helped him out of the trunk of the car and led him

over to the entrance of another cave. Normalcy was returning and Jurgen began thinking how he was going to get hold of the guy and make sure he didn't repeat whatever it was he had done to him.

The man said, "Walk on over to the front of the cave in front of that sign that has the Soldano logo on it and I want you to tell me about raping and killing the woman who used to live on the hog farm."

Jurgen judged the distance between them, then noticed the man held some device in the hand he had used to point a finger at him and zap him with some electrical charge. The bastard had one of those tazers, that's what it was. If he could get hold of it he would stick it up the man's ass.

The man pointed, "Over there, remember?"

Jurgen didn't have much choice at the moment. He would find a way to get to the man before he zapped him again, he was sure of that. Hell, the man had no idea who he was screwing around with or what Jurgen was capable of. He walked to the spot the man pointed out and turned around. Still too far away. Just wait. The guy would make a mistake. Jurgen just needed a second to get the upper hand.

"Now," the man said, "I want you to tell me about the woman. How you raped her and killed her."

Who the hell was this guy and what was he up to. Only one thing Jurgen could think of, the guy wanted to blackmail him. So, play along with the bastard, watch for the opening he was sure would come and he would end the guy's scheme real quick.

Jurgen grinned, trying to make it as bad a grin as he could, like the cage fighter on his bicep standing over his downed opponent. "Yeah, the old woman. She wasn't that bad, actually. I don't think she's had anybody inside her for a while. She squealed for a minute or two. Wouldn't sign the damn paper I had and I tapped her pretty hard I guess. So, I had to finish her."

"That's enough," the man said. "I got it on the camera over there on the tripod."

"You son of a bitch," Jurgen said and started for him, almost got to him before the man pointed at his crotch and his testicles seemed to explode and a fire started there that actually made him scream. He grabbed his crotch, held, squeezed, and felt tears of pain coming down his cheeks. He fell to his knees, bent over in pain. He heard the man talking to him, heard his words, couldn't believe what he was saying.

"You probably still have the knife you used on her. I want you to take it out and cut off a couple of your toes."

"What? What?" the man's words didn't make sense to him.

"Take off a shoe. You can make the choice which foot. Take off a shoe and cut off two toes."

The world became surreal. Jurgen didn't even know what was happening anymore. He was like an observer. Someone had a knife in their hand, someone put a blade of the knife against his foot and Jurgen was saying, "Please, mister, please. What the hell are you doing to me. Don't make me do this," and the man's face was in his face and the man said, "I want you to feel the pain she felt when you sliced open her throat," and Jurgen screamed, "Daddy, Daddy, help me," as his little toe dropped off his foot and he saw the blood flow and saw that the hand holding the knife was his own hand and he screamed and fell backwards.

When he woke he was holding the maroon T-shirt with the sleeves ripped off on his throbbing foot. He realized he must be inside the dark cave. And it smelled like pig shit.

36

Ev Miehle liked driving his own car. When he was busy or didn't know where in the hell someplace was, the limo was convenient. But nothing like getting your hands on the steering wheel of a damn good automobile. The teenage boy in him came out like the boy who had tooled the '49 Studebaker convertible around many years ago.

He pulled into the Soldano executive parking garage, the attendant waving him on through just by recognizing the Ferrari, no checking credentials. He drove into the first spot—his spot with his name on it, noticed the space next to his, Marla's (damn, that woman could drive a bargain)—was empty and caused him to wonder where in the hell she could be in the middle of the day.

He noticed Jurgen's BMW in the spot next to Marla's and thought, "What's Jurgen doing here, he's supposed to be at the farm."

As he got out of the Ferrari—the door barely making a click when he closed it—a tall man got out of Jurgen's Beamer and walked toward him.

"Where's Jurgen?" Ev asked the man, not liking a stranger in the executive parking garage.

The man pulled a phone from his pocket, got something on the screen and turned it so Ev could see.

It was Jurgen, sitting on the ground in front of a limestone cave entrance—the Soldano logo on the sign behind him—cutting off his own toe and screaming, "Daddy, Daddy, help me."

"He needs you," the man said.

Ev Miehle was stunned. Rarely did he encounter a situation he couldn't handle in a heartbeat, but what the hell was this?

It took a moment to get it out before he said, "Who the hell are you? Where's my son?"

"As you can see, he's on the farm, by one of the caves where you dumped the radioactive material from the STOLID project. You might want to watch this, also."

Jurgen stood by the cave entrance looking defiant. He recited how he killed Cecilia Roth and the pleasure he took in it was apparent. Ev Miehle watched speechless. His mouth was dry and thoughts churned in his head. Stocks and bonds and bottom lines he calculated instantly, but this?

"Here's the deal, Ev. I'm going to give you some choices here. Marla coughed up the STOLID file from the FDA. The one she had expunged in exchange for a parking space next to yours and a plush office, stocks and a salary better even than Jurgen's. But, she went off to buy a strapless bikini for a beach somewhere."

"Who the hell are you?" Ev repeated.

"Consider me the competition. You need a name, call me Lucky."

"DuPont," Ev spat out. "Those sons of bitches. This is war. I'll get you bastards for this."

"Right now Ev, I think you ought to be concerned about your son."

'Where is my son. Goddammit, if you've hurt him you're done for, Mister."

"Well, he hurt himself, actually. Right now, he's inside the cave, but don't worry, if you cooperate I'm going to give you a chance to get him out. We'll have to make it quick, of course. A day or two inside an underground cave filled with radioactive material and pig shit may not be too pleasant."

"You're a dead man," Ev said, not the Good Ol' boy voice, but a voice executives around a boardroom table learned to fear.

"You're not the first man to tell me that, Ev, but here I am. Now, let's get down to business. I worked out an executive order to present to the board of directors. Once the FDA report is made public, unlike my offer to you, they won't have too many choices about approving your order. "

"Get on with it," Ev said. He started to open his briefcase, but the man took it from him.

"Didn't want you to push the panic button on your phone inside here. It makes such a racket. Okay, here's the gist of the executive order. First, you close the farm and get rid of the hogs. Next you pay to clean the place up and clean out all the caves. I don't have any idea what the Department of Natural Resources is going to do with you about that, but they will give you instructions on how to clean the mess up. You're going to deed the acreage of the farm to the state for a state park to be named the Cecilia Roth State Park. You're going to give one million dollars each to the estates of the seven people who were murdered to establish the farm. That 501C4 or whatever its supposed to be, you know the one you've been using to make all those political contributions, the one that has a hundred and twenty-seven million dollars in it, give or take a few bucks, well, you're going to give that to cancer research and to the local hospitals and the ones in St. Louis where the workers you poisoned were treated."

The Special Edition

"And you think I'm going to sign this?"

"I'm giving you a choice, Ev. You don't have to sign it, you can just leave Jurgen inside that radioactive cave living off poisoned grain and pig shit. He's got a bad foot so he needs somebody to help him."

"You're a son of a bitch."

"You're repeating yourself, Ev. But consider, I haven't raped and murdered any women and I haven't left several hundred people with cancer, if you want to compare records."

Ev Miehle breathed deeply. He looked around. He thought the security man at the door to the garage carried a pistol. He could yell out, but the bastard might have his own pistol and use it. And Jurgen would die in the damn cave. He'd always had bad feelings about the damn caves. At first they seemed like a good idea, someplace to get rid of the stuff they didn't want the FDA or anyone else finding. And the smell of all the manure in the caves and all over the farm kept curiosity seekers away.

He needed time, but the man wasn't giving him any. "Let me see the damn thing," he said and the man handed him an iPad. He looked on the screen, started reading, growing angrier with each word. He finished reading, saw a space for his signature at the end. "Where do I sign?" he asked. The man handed him a silver scroll pad and a funny looking pen. He scrawled his name on the pad and saw it appear on the screen. The man took the iPad, punched some keys and closed it.

"Done," he said. "Went directly to your CEO site and on to all the executives and to your brother. And, of course, to the media and to the Justice Department. Now, what we'll do is I'll drive you out to the cave where I left Jurgen. I'll unlock it and you can go in and help your son. You won't be able to come back out the way you go in. There is a way through the underground passage-way to other exits that are not locked. You may have to wade up to your waist in pig shit and make your way through the radioac-tive material you dumped there, but if you hurry I think you can find your way out."

"Thought I had a choice."

"Oh, you do. You can just leave Jurgen in there to fend for himself. He's a big boy."

"I'm going to kill you for this."

"Hire somebody good, Ev. Because if they fail, I'll come looking for you. That is, if you find your way out of the caves."

Ev Miehle stood immobile. His eyes looked off in the dis-tance as if looking at the future and not liking what he saw.

"Let's go," he said. They got in the BMW and drove away.

Serena sat at her new desk with her left arm in a sling and a scarf around her head to cover up the spot of hair that had been shaved for her brain scan. Cooper looked at her, at her sling, and said, "How you going to do the ads you sold with one hand?"

"I hired Jimmy Rodriquez. He comes in at one to do the graphics."

"And you hired him because you are the . . .?"

"Owner," she said. "Part owner, you said when you tried to return the money to my parents."

"That's true, but when we get married you will be the full owner. Along with me, of course."

"We can make joint decisions, then."

"Yes, we can. I bought a new double wide mobile home."

"And you bought it because you are the. . .?"

"Owner. Part owner, actually."

"I ordered a reprint on this week's paper. We sold out an hour after the paper was delivered." She had a smug look on her face.

"That's good. We are the only newspaper in the county now with the *Carrier* closing shop. We'll need to hire more people. And double the press run."

"It worked out well, didn't it? First Mister Graham tells the whole scam before he shoots himself, then we tell it all again, only this time we've got proof." She seemed very pleased with her revelation.

Cooper said, "Well, we had some luck and a lot of help. Jimmy not being the least. How much are you paying him?"

"He doesn't know how much we're paying him. Sort of like someone else who was hired here."

Cooper grinned at her. "I'm a lucky guy."

He looked out the window and saw a tall, well dressed man coming up the walk. He smiled and waited for the man to come inside. The man stood and looked the place over and came over to Cooper who had a hand outstretched.

"Hello, Dad," he said. "Good to see you again."

"Son, you haven't changed much. I read your *Special Edition* at the convenience store coming into town. Good looking paper. Lots of news."

"Thanks to all the good help I've been getting."

"You solved the murder of your mother," the man said. "That's good. I loved her once, too, you know."

"I remember." The last of childhood animosities evaporated.

"Dad, I'd like you to meet Serena Gonzalez. Soon to be Serena Rease."

Cooper's father took Serena's hand and held it for a moment. "Nice to meet you Serena. You will make a beautiful addition to our family."

Cooper said, "My Dad, Serena. Gerald Rease. Some call him Lucky. You can call him Parker."

—30—

www.ingramcontent.com/pod-product-compliance
Lightning Source LLC
Chambersburg PA
CBHW021040130626
46552CB00005B/1948